TALES
OF THE
WEIRD

TALES
OF THE
WEIRD

An Uncanny Introduction

BRITISH LIBRARY

This collection first published in 2023 by
The British Library
96 Euston Road
London NW1 2DB

Volume © 2023 The British Library Board

'"He Made a Woman –"' © 1923 Marjorie Bowen. Reprinted
with permission of the Estate of Gabrielle Long.

'Celui-Là' © 1929 Eleanor Scott. Reprinted with permission
of the Estate of Helen Magdalen Leys.

'The Visiting Star' © 1966 Robert Aickman. Reprinted
with the permission of Artellus Limited.

Dates attributed to each story relate to first publication.

ISBN 978 0 7123 5499 8

Frontispiece photograph by Fay Godwin © The British Library Board.
As featured in the British Library edition of *Randalls Round*.

Cover design by Mauricio Villamayor with illustration by Enrique Bernardou
Text design and typesetting by Tetragon, London

www.bl.uk/publishing

🐦 ♪ 📷 @bl_publishing

CONTENTS

INTRODUCTION

The Tales of the Weird series has been continually growing and reviving long-lost material from the British Library's vaults for almost five years now – bringing back to print an exhilarating array of uncanny story-telling from the realms of gothic, supernatural and horror fiction. With stories ranging from the nineteenth century to the present day, master editors explore the horrific potential of topics such as fiendish flora, blood-curdling bugs and the unequivocally sinister side of the festive season – from authors both beloved and overlooked.

Tales of the Weird: An Uncanny Introduction brings together a chilling collection of stories from across the entire series, offering a brief insight into the abyssal depths of the British Library archives – with offerings by Eleanor Scott, Robert Aickman, William Hope Hodgson and Vernon Lee.

MARSYAS IN FLANDERS

Vernon Lee

Vernon Lee was the nom de plume of Violet Paget (1856–1935), a British author and essayist, outspoken in her feminist and pacifist views and relationships with other women. She lived much of her life in Europe, immersed in artistic and literary traditions which would influence her pioneering work in the Aesthetic movement and her stunningly original fiction. From the modernised folktales "Marsyas in Flanders" and "The Legend of Madame Krasinska" to ingenious psychological hauntings such as "A Phantom Lover" and "Amour Dure", Lee's captivating voice rings out just as distinctively now as in her fin-de-siècle heyday.

"ou are right. This is not the original crucifix at all. Another one has been put instead. *Il y a eu substitution*," and the little old Antiquary of Dunes nodded mysteriously, fixing his ghostseer's eyes upon mine.

He said it in a scarce audible whisper. For it happened to be the vigil of the Feast of the Crucifix, and the once famous church was full of semi-clerical persons decorating it for the morrow, and of old ladies in strange caps, clattering about with pails and brooms. The Antiquary had brought me there the very moment of my arrival, lest the crowd of faithful should prevent his showing me everything next morning.

The famous crucifix was exhibited behind rows and rows of unlit candles, and surrounded by strings of paper flowers and coloured muslin, and garlands of sweet resinous maritime pine; and two lighted chandeliers illumined it.

"There has been an exchange," he repeated, looking round that no one might hear him. "*Il y a eu substitution*."

For I had remarked, as anyone would have done, at the first glance, that the crucifix had every appearance of French work of the thirteenth century, boldly realistic, whereas the crucifix of the legend, which was a work of St. Luke, which had hung for centuries in the Holy Sepulchre at Jerusalem and been miraculously cast ashore at Dunes in 1195, would surely have been a more or less Byzantine image, like its miraculous companion of Lucca.

"But why should there have been a substitution?" I inquired innocently.

"Hush, hush," answered the Antiquary, frowning, "not here—later, later—"

He took me all over the church, once so famous for pilgrimages; but from which, even like the sea which has left it in a salt marsh beneath the cliffs, the tide of devotion has receded for centuries. It is a very dignified little church, of charmingly restrained and shapely Gothic, built of a delicate pale stone, which the sea damp has picked out, in bases and capitals and carved foliation, with stains of a lovely bright green. The Antiquary showed me where the transept and belfry had been left unfinished when the miracles had diminished in the fourteenth century. And he took me up to the curious warder's chamber, a large room up some steps in the triforium; with a fireplace and stone seats for the men who guarded the precious crucifix day and night. There had even been beehives in the window, he told me, and he remembered seeing them still as a child.

"Was it usual, here in Flanders, to have a guardroom in churches containing important relics?" I asked, for I could not remember having seen anything similar before.

"By no means," he answered, looking round to make sure we were alone, "but it was necessary here. You have never heard in what the chief miracles of this church consisted?"

"No," I whispered back, gradually infected by his mysteriousness, "unless you allude to the legend that the figure of the Saviour broke all the crosses until the right one was cast up by the sea?"

He shook his head but did not answer, and descended the steep stairs into the nave, while I lingered a moment looking down into it from the warder's chamber. I have never had so curious an impression of a church. The chandeliers on either side of the crucifix swirled slowly round, making great pools of light which were broken by the shadows of the clustered columns, and among the pews of the nave moved the flicker of the sacristan's lamp. The place was full of the scent of resinous pine branches, evoking dunes and mountain-sides; and from the busy groups below rose a subdued chatter of women's voices, and a splash of water and clatter of pattens. It vaguely suggested preparations for a witches' sabbath.

"What sort of miracles did they have in this church?" I asked, when we had passed into the dusky square, "and what did you mean about their having exchanged the crucifix—about a *substitution?*"

It seemed quite dark outside. The church rose black, a vague lopsided mass of buttresses and high-pitched roofs, against the watery, moonlit sky; the big trees of the churchyard behind waving about in the seawind; and the windows shone yellow, like flaming portals, in the darkness.

"Please remark the bold effect of the gargoyles," said the Antiquary pointing upwards.

They jutted out, vague wild beasts, from the roof-line; and, what was positively frightening, you saw the moonlight, yellow and blue through the open jaws of some of them. A gust swept through the trees, making the weathercock clatter and groan.

"Why, those gargoyle wolves seem positively to howl," I exclaimed.

The old Antiquary chuckled. "Aha," he answered, "did I not tell you that this church has witnessed things like no other church in Christendom? And it still remembers them! There—have you ever known such a wild, savage church before?"

And as he spoke there suddenly mingled with the sough of the wind and the groans of the weather-vane, a shrill quavering sound as of pipers inside.

"The organist trying his *vox humana* for tomorrow," remarked the Antiquary.

II

Next day I bought one of the printed histories of the miraculous crucifix which they were hawking all round the church; and next day also, my friend the Antiquary was good enough to tell me all that he knew of the matter. Between my two informants, the following may be said to be the true story.

In the autumn of 1195, after a night of frightful storm, a boat was found cast upon the shore of Dunes, which was at that time a fishing village at the mouth of the Nys, and exactly opposite a terrible sunken reef.

The boat was broken and upset; and close to it, on the sand and bent grass, lay a stone figure of the crucified Saviour, without its cross and, as seems probable, also without its arms, which had been made of separate blocks. A variety of persons immediately came forward to claim it; the little church of Dunes, on whose glebe it was found; the Barons of Croÿ, who had the right of jetsam on that coast, and also the great Abbey of St. Loup of Arras, as possessing the spiritual overlordship of the place. But a holy man who lived close by in the cliffs, had a vision which settled the dispute. St. Luke in person appeared and told him that he was the original maker of the figure; that it had been one of three which had hung round the Holy Sepulchre of Jerusalem; that three knights, a Norman, a Tuscan,

14

and a man of Arras, had with the permission of Heaven stolen them from the Infidels and placed them on unmanned boats; that one of the images had been cast upon the Norman coast near Salenelles; that the second had run aground not far from the city of Lucca, in Italy; and that this third was the one which had been embarked by the knight from Artois. As regarded its final resting place, the hermit, on the authority of St. Luke, recommended that the statue should be left to decide the matter itself. Accordingly, the crucified figure was solemnly cast back into the sea. The very next day it was found once more in the same spot, among the sand and bent grass at the mouth of the Nys. It was therefore deposited in the little church of Dunes; and very soon indeed the flocks of pious persons who brought it offerings from all parts made it necessary and possible to rebuild the church thus sanctified by its presence.

The Holy Effigy of Dunes—*Sacra Dunarum Effigies* as it was called— did not work the ordinary sort of miracles. But its fame spread far and wide by the unexampled wonders which became the constant accompaniment of its existence. The Effigy, as above mentioned, had been discovered without the cross to which it had evidently been fastened, nor had any researches or any subsequent storms brought the missing blocks to light, despite the many prayers which were offered for the purpose. After some time, therefore, and a deal of discussion, it was decided that a new cross should be provided for the effigy to hang upon. And certain skilful stonemasons of Arras were called to Dunes for this purpose. But behold! the very day after the cross had been solemnly erected in the church, an unheard of and terrifying fact was discovered. The Effigy, which had been hanging perfectly straight the previous evening, had shifted its position, and was bent violently to the right, as if in an effort to break loose.

This was attested not merely by hundreds of laymen, but by the priests of the place, who notified the fact in a document, existing in the episcopal archives of Arras until 1790, to the Abbot of St. Loup their spiritual overlord.

This was the beginning of a series of mysterious occurrences which spread the fame of the marvellous crucifix all over Christendom. The Effigy did not remain in the position into which it had miraculously worked itself: it was found, at intervals of time, shifted in some other manner upon its cross, and always as if it had gone through violent contortions. And one day, about ten years after it had been cast up by the sea, the priests of the church and the burghers of Dunes discovered the Effigy hanging in its original outstretched, symmetrical attitude, but, O wonder! with the cross, broken in three pieces, lying on the steps of its chapel.

Certain persons, who lived in the end of the town nearest the church, reported to have been roused in the middle of the night by what they had taken for a violent clap of thunder, but which was doubtless the crash of the cross falling down; or perhaps, who knows? the noise with which the terrible Effigy had broken loose and spurned the alien cross from it. For that was the secret: the Effigy, made by a saint and come to Dunes by miracle, had evidently found some trace of unholiness in the stone to which it had been fastened. Such was the ready explanation afforded by the Prior of the church, in answer to an angry summons of the Abbot of St. Loup, who expressed his disapproval of such unusual miracles. Indeed, it was discovered that the piece of marble had not been cleaned from sinful human touch with the necessary rites before the figure was fastened on; a most grave, though excusable oversight. So a new cross was ordered, although it was noticed that much time was lost about it; and the consecration took place only some years later.

Meanwhile the Prior had built the warder's chamber, with the fireplace and recess, and obtained permission from the Pope himself that a clerk in orders should watch day and night, on the score that so wonderful a relic might be stolen. For the relic had by this time entirely cut out all similar crucifixes, and the village of Dunes, through the concourse of pilgrims, had rapidly grown into a town, the property of the now fabulously wealthy Priory of the Holy Cross.

The Abbots of St. Loup, however, looked upon the matter with an unfavourable eye. Although nominally remaining their vassals, the Priors of Dunes had contrived to obtain gradually from the Pope privileges which rendered them virtually independent, and in particular, immunities which sent to the treasury of St. Loup only a small proportion of the tribute money brought by the pilgrims. Abbot Walterius in particular, showed himself actively hostile. He accused the Prior of Dunes of having employed his warders to trump up stories of strange movements and sounds on the part of the still crossless Effigy, and of suggesting, to the ignorant, changes in its attitude which were more credulously believed in now that there was no longer the straight line of the cross by which to verify. So finally the new cross was made, and consecrated, and on Holy Cross Day of the year, the Effigy was fastened to it in the presence of an immense concourse of clergy and laity. The Effigy, it was now supposed, would be satisfied, and no unusual occurrences would increase or perhaps fatally compromise its reputation for sanctity.

These expectations were violently dispelled. In November, 1293, after a year of strange rumours concerning the Effigy, the figure was again discovered to have moved, and continued moving, or rather (judging from the position on the cross) writhing; and on Christmas Eve of the same year, the cross was a second time thrown down and dashed in pieces. The priest on duty was, at the same time, found, it was thought, dead, in his warder's chamber. Another cross was made and this time privately consecrated and put in place, and a hole in the roof made a pretext to close the church for a while, and to perform the rites of purification necessary after its pollution by workmen. Indeed, it was remarked that on this occasion the Prior of Dunes took as much trouble to diminish and if possible to hide away the miracles, as his predecessor had done his best to blazon the preceding ones abroad. The priest who had been on duty on the eventful Christmas Eve disappeared mysteriously, and it was thought by many persons that he had gone mad and was confined in the Prior's prison, for fear of the revelations he might make. For by this time, and not without some encouragement from the Abbots at Arras, extraordinary stories had begun to circulate about the goings-on in the church of Dunes. This church, be it remembered, stood a little above the town, isolated and surrounded by big trees. It was surrounded by the precincts of the Priory and, save on the water side, by high walls. Nevertheless, persons there were who affirmed that, the wind having been in that direction, they had heard strange noises come from the church of nights. During storms, particularly, sounds had been heard which were variously described as howls, groans, and the music of rustic dancing. A master mariner affirmed that one Hallow Even, as his boat approached the mouth of the Nys, he had seen the church of Dunes brilliantly lit up, its immense windows flaming. But he was suspected of being drunk and of having exaggerated the effect of the small light shining from the warder's chamber. The interest of the townfolk of Dunes coincided with that of the Priory, since they prospered greatly by the pilgrimages, so these tales were promptly hushed up. Yet they undoubtedly reached the ear of the Abbot of St. Loup. And at last there came an event which brought them all back to the surface.

For, on the Vigil of All Saints, 1299, the church was struck by lightning. The new warder was found dead in the middle of the nave, the cross broken in two; and oh, horror! the Effigy was missing. The indescribable fear which overcame every one was merely increased by the discovery of the Effigy lying behind the high altar, in an attitude of frightful convulsion, and, it was whispered, blackened by lightning.

This was the end of the strange doings at Dunes.

An ecclesiastical council was held at Arras, and the church shut once more for nearly a year. It was opened this time and reconsecrated by the Abbot of St. Loup, whom the Prior of Holy Cross served humbly at mass. A new chapel had been built, and in it the miraculous crucifix was displayed, dressed in more splendid brocade and gems than usual, and its head nearly hidden by one of the most gorgeous crowns ever seen before; a gift, it was said, of the Duke of Burgundy.

All this new splendour, and the presence of the great Abbot himself, was presently explained to the faithful, when the Prior came forward to announce that a last and greatest miracle had now taken place. The original cross, on which the figure had hung in the Church of the Holy Sepulchre, and for which the Effigy had spurned all others made by less holy hands, had been cast on the shore of Dunes, on the very spot where, a hundred years before, the figure of the Saviour had been discovered in the sands. "This," said the

Prior, "was the explanation of the terrible occurrences which had filled all hearts with anguish. The Holy Effigy was now satisfied, it would rest in peace and its miraculous powers would be engaged only in granting the prayers of the faithful."

One-half of the forecast came true: from that day forward the Effigy never shifted its position; but from that day forward also, no considerable miracle was ever registered; the devotion of Dunes diminished, other relics threw the Sacred Effigy into the shade; and the pilgrimages dwindling to mere local gatherings, the church was never brought to completion.

What had happened? No one ever knew, guessed, or perhaps even asked. But, when in 1790 the Archiepiscopal palace of Arras was sacked, a certain notary of the neighbourhood bought a large portion of the archives at the price of waste paper, either from historical curiosity, or expecting to obtain thereby facts which might gratify his aversion to the clergy. These documents lay unexamined for many years, till my friend the Antiquary bought them. Among them, taken helter skelter from the Archbishop's palace, were sundry papers referring to the suppressed Abbey of St. Loup of Arras, and among these latter, a series of notes concerning the affairs of the church of Dunes; they were, so far as their fragmentary nature explained, the minutes of an inquest made in 1309, and contained the deposition of sundry witnesses. To understand their meaning it is necessary to remember that this was the time when witch trials had begun, and when the proceedings against the Templars had set the fashion of inquests which could help the finances of the country while furthering the interests of religion.

What appears to have happened is that after the catastrophe of the Vigil of All Saints, October, 1299, the Prior, Urbain de Luc, found himself suddenly threatened with a charge of sacrilege and witchcraft, of obtaining the miracles of the Effigy by devilish means, and of converting his church into a chapel of the Evil One.

Instead of appealing to high ecclesiastical tribunals, as the privileges obtained from the Holy See would have warranted, Prior Urbain guessed that this charge came originally from the wrathful Abbey of St. Loup, and, dropping all his pretensions in order to save himself, he threw himself upon the mercy of the Abbot whom he had hitherto flouted. The Abbot appears, to have been satisfied by his submission, and the matter to have dropped after a few legal preliminaries, of which the notes found among the archiepiscopal archives of Arras represented a portion. Some of these notes my friend the Antiquary kindly allowed me to translate from the Latin, and I give them here, leaving the reader to make what he can of them.

"Item. The Abbot expresses himself satisfied that His Reverence the Prior has had no personal knowledge of or dealings with the Evil One (*Diabolus*). Nevertheless, the gravity of the charge requires..."— here the page is torn.

"Hugues Jacquot, Simon le Couvreur, Pierre Denis, burghers of Dunes, being interrogated, witness:

"That the noises from the Church of the Holy Cross always happened on nights of bad storms, and foreboded shipwrecks on the coast; and were very various, such as terrible rattling, groans, howls as of wolves, and occasional flute playing. A certain Jehan, who has twice been branded and flogged for lighting fires on the coast and otherwise causing ships to wreck at the mouth of the Nys, being promised immunity, after two or three slight pulls on the rack,

21

witnesses as follows: That the band of wreckers to which he belongs always knew when a dangerous storm was brewing, on account of the noises which issued from the church of Dunes. Witness has often climbed the walls and prowled round in the churchyard, waiting to hear such noises. He was not unfamiliar with the howlings and roarings mentioned by the previous witnesses. He has heard tell by a countryman who passed in the night that the howling was such that the countryman thought himself pursued by a pack of wolves, although it is well known that no wolf has been seen in these parts for thirty years. But the witness himself is of opinion that the most singular of all the noises, and the one which always accompanied or foretold the worst storms, was a noise of flutes and pipes (*quod vulgo dicuntur flustes et musettes*) so sweet that the King of France could not have sweeter at his Court. Being interrogated whether he had ever seen anything? the witness answers: 'That he has seen the church brightly lit up from the sands; but on approaching found all dark, save the light from the warder's chamber. That once, by moonlight, the piping and fluting and howling being uncommonly loud, he thought he had seen wolves, and a human figure on the roof, but that he ran away from fear, and cannot be sure.'

"Item. His Lordship the Abbot desires the Right Reverend Prior to answer truly, placing his hand on the Gospels, whether or not he had himself heard such noises.

"The Right Reverend Prior denies ever having heard anything similar. But, being threatened with further proceedings (the rack?) acknowledges that he had frequently been told of these noises by the Warder on duty.

"*Query:* Whether the Right Reverend Prior was ever told anything else by the Warder?

"*Answer:* Yes; but under the seal of confession. The last Warder, moreover, the one killed by lightning, had been a reprobate priest, having committed the greatest crimes and obliged to take asylum, whom the Prior had kept there on account of the difficulty of finding a man sufficiently courageous for the office.

"*Query:* Whether the Prior has ever questioned previous Warders?

"*Answer:* That the Warders were bound to reveal only in confession whatever they had heard; that the Prior's predecessors had kept the seal of confession inviolate, and that though unworthy, the Prior himself desired to do alike.

"*Query:* What had become of the Warder who had been found in a swoon after the occurrences of Hallow Even?

"*Answer:* That the Prior does not know. The Warder was crazy. The Prior believes he was secluded for that reason."

A disagreeable surprise had been, apparently, arranged for Prior Urbain de Luc. For the next entry states that:

"Item. By order of His Magnificence the Lord Abbot, certain servants of the Lord Abbot aforesaid introduce Robert Baudouin, priest, once Warder in the Church of the Holy Cross, who has been kept ten years in prison by His Reverence the Prior, as being of unsound mind. Witness manifests great terror on finding himself in the presence of their Lordships, and particularly of His Reverence the Prior. And refuses to speak, hiding his face in his hands and uttering shrieks. Being comforted with kind words by those present, nay even most graciously by My Lord the Abbot himself, *etiam* threatened with the rack if he continue obdurate, this witness deposes as follows, not without much lamentation, shrieking and senseless jabber after the manner of mad men.

"*Query:* Can he remember what happened on the Vigil of All Saints, in the church of Dunes, before he swooned on the floor of the church?

"*Answer:* He cannot. It would be sin to speak of such things before great spiritual Lords. Moreover he is but an ignorant man, and also mad. Moreover his hunger is great.

"Being given white bread from the Lord Abbot's own table, witness is again cross-questioned.

"*Query:* What can he remember of the events of the Vigil of All Saints?

"*Answer:* Thinks he was not always mad. Thinks he has not always been in prison. Thinks he once went in a boat on sea, etc.

"*Query:* Does witness think he has ever been in the church of Dunes?

"*Answer:* Cannot remember. But is sure that he was not always in prison.

"*Query:* Has witness ever heard anything like that? (My Lord the Abbot having secretly ordered that a certain fool in his service, an excellent musician, should suddenly play the pipes behind the Arras.)

"At which sound witness began to tremble and sob and fall on his knees, and catch hold of the robe even of My Lord the Abbot, hiding his head therein.

"*Query:* Wherefore does he feel such terror, being in the fatherly presence of so clement a prince as the Lord Abbot?

"*Answer:* That witness cannot stand that piping any longer. That it freezes his blood. That he has told the Prior many times that he will not remain any longer in the warder's chamber. That he is afraid for his life. That he dare not make the sign of the Cross nor say his prayers for fear of the Great Wild Man. That the Great Wild Man took the Cross and broke it in two and played at quoits with it in the nave. That all the wolves trooped down from the roof howling, and danced on their hind legs while the Great Wild Man played the pipes on the high altar. That witness had surrounded himself with a hedge of little crosses, made of broken rye straw, to keep off the Great Wild Man from the warder's chamber. Ah—ah—ah! He is piping again! The wolves are howling! He is raising the tempest.

"*Item*. That no further information can be extracted from witness, who falls on the floor like one possessed and has to be removed from the presence of His Lordship the Abbot and His Reverence the Prior."

III

Here the minutes of the inquest break off. Did those great spiritual dignitaries ever get to learn more about the terrible doings in the church of Dunes? Did they ever guess at their cause?

"For there was a cause," said the Antiquary, folding his spectacles after reading me these notes, "or more strictly the cause still exists. And you will understand, though those learned priests of six centuries ago could not."

And rising, he fetched a key from a shelf and preceded me into the yard of his house, situated on the Nys, a mile below Dunes.

Between the low steadings one saw the salt marsh, lilac with sea lavender, the Island of Birds, a great sandbank at the mouth of the Nys, where every kind of sea fowl gathers; and beyond, the angry white-crested sea under an angry orange afterglow. On the other side, inland, and appearing above the farm roofs, stood the church of

Dunes, its pointed belfry and jagged outlines of gables and buttresses and gargoyles and wind-warped pines black against the easterly sky of ominous livid red.

"I told you," said the Antiquary, stopping with the key in the lock of a big outhouse, "that there had been a *substitution*; that the crucifix at present at Dunes is not the one miraculously cast up by the storm of 1195. I believe the present one may be identified as a life-size statue, for which a receipt exists in the archives of Arras, furnished to the Abbot of St. Loup by Estienne Le Mas and Guillaume Pernel, stone masons, in the year 1299, that is to say the year of the inquest and of the cessation of all supernatural occurrences at Dunes. As to the original effigy, you shall see it and understand everything."

The Antiquary opened the door of a sloping, vaulted passage, lit a lantern and led the way. It was evidently the cellar of some mediæval building; and a scent of wine, of damp wood, and of fir branches from innumerable stacked up faggots, filled the darkness among thickset columns.

"Here," said the Antiquary, raising his lantern, "he was buried beneath this vault, and they had run an iron stake through his middle, like a vampire, to prevent his rising."

The Effigy was erect against the dark wall, surrounded by brushwood. It was more than life-size, nude, the arms broken off at the shoulders, the head, with stubbly beard and clotted hair, drawn up with an effort, the face contracted with agony; the muscles dragged as of one hanging crucified, the feet bound together with a rope. The figure was familiar to me in various galleries. I came forward to examine the ear: it was leaf-shaped.

"Ah, you have understood the whole mystery," said the Antiquary.

"I have understood," I answered, not knowing how far his thought really went, "that this supposed statue of Christ is an antique satyr, a Marsyas awaiting his punishment."

The Antiquary nodded. "Exactly," he said drily, "that is the whole explanation. Only I think the Abbot and the Prior were not so wrong to drive the iron stake through him when they removed him from the church."

THE VOICE IN THE NIGHT

William Hope Hodgson

This tale by essayist, novelist and short-story writer William Hope Hodgson first appeared in *The Blue Book* magazine's November 1907 issue. Known for his nautical themes, he drew upon his own experiences at sea from a young age as a cabin boy. As an accomplished horror writer, his short story "The Voice in the Night" is one of the eeriest in the collection. The story begins one night as a schooner is approached by a small rowboat in distress but it is too dark to see the man inside. He tells them of his tragic tale and pleas for some supplies to take back for his fiancée. This story is different to the others as it features fungi and not a flower, vine or tree. However, in terms of man-eating/parasitic plant horror and science fiction, fungi are part of the same narrative and share symbolism as the immobile become mobile and the food sources become the hunters. The all-consuming fungus stems from the same fear of contagion and infection as the modern zombie narrative, including cannibalistic elements as the victims of the fungus experience insatiable and indiscriminate hunger.

t was a dark, starless night. We were becalmed in the Northern Pacific. Our exact position I do not know; for the sun had been hidden during the course of a weary, breathless week, by a thin haze which had seemed to float above us, about the height of our mastheads, at whiles descending and shrouding the surrounding sea.

With there being no wind, we had steadied the tiller, and I was the only man on deck. The crew, consisting of two men and a boy, were sleeping forrard in their den; while Will—my friend, and the master of our little craft—was aft in his bunk on the port side of the little cabin.

Suddenly, from out of the surrounding darkness, there came a hail:

"Schooner, ahoy!"

The cry was so unexpected that I gave no immediate answer, because of my surprise.

It came again—a voice curiously throaty and inhuman, calling from somewhere upon the dark sea away on our port broadside:

"Schooner, ahoy!"

"Hullo!" I sung out, having gathered my wits somewhat. "What are you? What do you want?"

"You need not be afraid," answered the queer voice, having probably noticed some trace of confusion in my tone. "I am only an old—man."

The pause sounded oddly; but it was only afterwards that it came back to me with any significance.

"Why don't you come alongside, then?" I queried somewhat snappishly; for I liked not his hinting at my having been a trifle shaken.

"I—I—can't. It wouldn't be safe. I—" The voice broke off, and there was silence.

"What do you mean?" I asked, growing more and more astonished. "Why not safe? Where are you?"

I listened for a moment; but there came no answer. And then, a sudden indefinite suspicion, of I knew not what, coming to me, I stepped swiftly to the binnacle, and took out the lighted lamp. At the same time, I knocked on the deck with my heel to waken Will. Then I was back at the side, throwing the yellow funnel of light out into the silent immensity beyond our rail. As I did so, I heard a slight, muffled cry, and then the sound of a splash, as though someone had dipped oars abruptly. Yet I cannot say that I saw anything with certainty; save, it seemed to me, that with the first flash of the light, there had been something upon the waters, where now there was nothing.

"Hullo, there!" I called. "What foolery is this!"

But there came only the indistinct sounds of a boat being pulled away into the night.

Then I heard Will's voice, from the direction of the after scuttle:

"What's up, George?"

"Come here, Will!" I said.

"What is it?" he asked, coming across the deck.

I told him the queer thing which had happened. He put several questions; then, after a moment's silence, he raised his hands to his lips, and hailed:

"Boat, ahoy!"

From a long distance away, there came back to us a faint reply, and my companion repeated his call. Presently, after a short period of silence, there grew on our hearing the muffled sound of oars; at which Will hailed again.

This time there was a reply:

"Put away the light."

"I'm damned if I will," I muttered; but Will told me to do as the voice bade, and I shoved it down under the bulwarks.

"Come nearer," he said, and the oar-strokes continued. Then, when apparently some half-dozen fathoms distant, they again ceased.

"Come alongside," exclaimed Will. "There's nothing to be frightened of aboard here!"

"Promise that you will not show the light?"

"What's to do with you," I burst out, "that you're so infernally afraid of the light?"

"Because——" began the voice, and stopped short.

"Because what?" I asked, quickly.

Will put his hand on my shoulder.

"Shut up a minute, old man," he said, in a low voice. "Let me tackle him."

He leant more over the rail.

"See here, Mister," he said, "this is a pretty queer business, you coming upon us like this, right out in the middle of the blessed Pacific. How are we to know what sort of a hanky-panky trick you're up to? You say there's only one of you. How are we to know, unless we get a squint at you—eh? What's your objection to the light, anyway?"

As he finished, I heard the noise of the oars again, and then the voice came; but now from a greater distance, and sounding extremely hopeless and pathetic.

"I am sorry—sorry! I would not have troubled you, only I am hungry, and—so is she."

The voice died away, and the sound of the oars, dipping irregularly, was borne to us.

"Stop!" sung out Will. "I don't want to drive you away. Come back! We'll keep the light hidden, if you don't like it."

He turned to me:

"It's a damned queer rig, this; but I think there's nothing to be afraid of?"

There was a question in his tone, and I replied.

"No, I think the poor devil's been wrecked around here, and gone crazy."

The sound of the oars drew nearer.

"Shove that lamp back in the binnacle," said Will; then he leaned over the rail, and listened. I replaced the lamp, and came back to his side. The dipping of the oars ceased some dozen yards distant.

"Won't you come alongside now?" asked Will in an even voice. "I have had the lamp put back in the binnacle."

"I—I cannot," replied the voice. "I dare not come nearer. I dare not even pay you for the—the provisions."

"That's all right," said Will, and hesitated. "You're welcome to as much grub as you can take—" Again he hesitated.

"You are very good," exclaimed the voice. "May God, Who understands everything, reward you—" It broke off huskily.

"The—the lady?" said Will, abruptly. "Is she—"

"I have left her behind upon the island," came the voice.

"What island?" I cut in.

"I know not its name," returned the voice. "I would to God—!" it began, and checked itself as suddenly.

"Could we not send a boat for her?" asked Will at this point.

"No!" said the voice, with extraordinary emphasis. "My God! No!" There was a moment's pause; then it added, in a tone which seemed a merited reproach:

"It was because of our want I ventured— Because her agony tortured me."

"I am a forgetful brute," exclaimed Will. "Just wait a minute, whoever you are, and I will bring you up something at once."

In a couple of minutes he was back again, and his arms were full of various edibles. He paused at the rail.

"Can't you come alongside for them?" he asked.

"No—I *dare not*," replied the voice, and it seemed to me that in its tones I detected a note of stifled craving—as though the owner hushed a mortal desire. It came to me then in a flash, that the poor old creature out there in the darkness, was *suffering* for actual need of that which Will held in his arms; and yet, because of some unintelligible dread, refraining from dashing to the side of our little schooner, and receiving it. And with the lightning-like conviction, there came the knowledge that the Invisible was not mad; but sanely facing some intolerable horror.

"Damn it, Will!" I said, full of many feelings, over which predominated a vast sympathy. "Get a box. We must float off the stuff to him in it."

This we did—propelling it away from the vessel, out into the darkness, by means of a boathook. In a minute, a slight cry from the Invisible came to us, and we knew that he had secured the box.

A little later, he called out a farewell to us, and so heartful a blessing, that I am sure we were the better for it. Then, without more ado, we heard the ply of oars across the darkness.

"Pretty soon off," remarked Will, with perhaps just a little sense of injury.

"Wait," I replied. "I think somehow he'll come back. He must have been badly needing that food."

"And the lady," said Will. For a moment he was silent; then he continued:

"It's the queerest thing ever I've tumbled across, since I've been fishing."

"Yes," I said, and fell to pondering.

And so the time slipped away—an hour, another, and still Will stayed with me; for the queer adventure had knocked all desire for sleep out of him.

The third hour was three parts through, when we heard again the sound of oars across the silent ocean.

"Listen!" said Will, a low note of excitement in his voice.

"He's coming, just as I thought," I muttered.

The dipping of the oars grew nearer, and I noted that the strokes were firmer and longer. The food had been needed.

They came to a stop a little distance off the broadside, and the queer voice came again to us through the darkness:

"Schooner, ahoy!"

"That you?" asked Will.

"Yes," replied the voice. "I left you suddenly; but—but there was great need."

"The lady?" questioned Will.

"The—lady is grateful now on earth. She will be more grateful soon in—in heaven."

Will began to make some reply, in a puzzled voice; but became confused, and broke off short. I said nothing. I was wondering at

36

the curious pauses, and, apart from my wonder, I was full of a great sympathy.

The voice continued:

"We—she and I, have talked, as we shared the result of God's tenderness and yours—"

Will interposed; but without coherence.

"I beg of you not to—to belittle your deed of Christian charity this night," said the voice. "Be sure that it has not escaped His notice."

It stopped, and there was a full minute's silence. Then it came again:

"We have spoken together upon that which—which has befallen us. We had thought to go out, without telling any, of the terror which has come into our—lives. She is with me in believing that tonight's happenings are under a special ruling, and that it is God's wish that we should tell to you all that we have suffered since—since—"

"Yes?" said Will, softly.

"Since the sinking of the *Albatross*."

"Ah!" I exclaimed, involuntarily. "She left Newcastle for 'Frisco some six months ago, and hasn't been heard of since."

"Yes," answered the voice. "But some few degrees to the North of the line she was caught in a terrible storm, and dismasted. When the day came, it was found that she was leaking badly, and, presently, it falling to a calm, the sailors took to the boats, leaving—leaving a young lady—my fiancée—and myself upon the wreck.

"We were below, gathering together a few of our belongings, when they left. They were entirely callous, through fear, and when we came up upon the decks, we saw them only as small shapes afar off upon the horizon. Yet we did not despair, but set to work and

37

constructed a small raft. Upon this we put such few matters as it would hold, including a quantity of water and some ship's biscuit. Then, the vessel being very deep in the water, we got ourselves onto the raft, and pushed off.

"It was later, when I observed that we seemed to be in the way of some tide or current, which bore us from the ship at an angle; so that in the course of three hours, by my watch, her hull became invisible to our sight, her broken masts remaining in view for a somewhat longer period. Then, towards evening, it grew misty, and so through the night. The next day we were still encompassed by the mist, the weather remaining quiet.

"For four days, we drifted through this strange haze, until, on the evening of the fourth day, there grew upon our ears the murmur of breakers at a distance. Gradually it became plainer, and, somewhat after midnight, it appeared to sound upon either hand at no very great space. The raft was raised upon a swell several times, and then we were in smooth water, and the noise of the breakers was behind.

"When the morning came, we found that we were in a sort of great lagoon; but of this we noticed little at the time; for close before us, through the enshrouding mist, loomed the hull of a large sailing-vessel. With one accord, we fell upon our knees and thanked God; for we thought that here was an end to our perils. We had much to learn.

"The raft drew near to the ship, and we shouted on them, to take us aboard; but none answered. Presently, the raft touched against the side of the vessel, and, seeing a rope hanging downwards, I seized it and began to climb. Yet I had much ado to make my way up, because of a kind of grey, lichenous fungus, which had seized upon the rope, and which blotched the side of the ship, lividly.

"I reached the rail, and clambered over it, on to the deck. Here, I saw that the decks were covered, in great patches, with the grey masses, some of them rising into nodules several feet in height; but at the time, I thought less of this matter than of the possibility of there being people aboard the ship. I shouted; but none answered. Then I went to the door below the poop-deck. I opened it, and peered in. There was a great smell of staleness, so that I knew in a moment that nothing living was within, and with the knowledge, I shut the door quickly; for I felt suddenly lonely.

"I went back to the side, where I had scrambled up. My—my sweetheart was still sitting quietly upon the raft. Seeing me look down, she called up to know whether there were any aboard of the ship. I replied that the vessel had the appearance of having been long deserted; but that if she would wait a little, I would see whether there was anything in the shape of a ladder, by which she could ascend to the deck. Then we would make a search through the vessel together. A little later, on the opposite side of the decks, I found a rope side-ladder. This I carried across, and a minute afterwards, she was beside me.

"Together, we explored the cabins and apartments in the after-part of the ship; but nowhere was there any sign of life. Here and there, within the cabins themselves, we came across odd patches of that queer fungus; but this, as my sweetheart said, could be cleansed away.

"In the end, having assured ourselves that the after portion of the vessel was empty, we picked our ways to the bows, between the ugly grey nodules of that strange growth; and here we made a further search, which told us that there was indeed none aboard but ourselves.

"This being now beyond any doubt, we returned to the stern of the ship, and proceeded to make ourselves as comfortable as possible. Together, we cleared out and cleaned two of the cabins; and, after that, I made examination whether there was anything eatable in the ship. This I soon found was so, and thanked God in my heart for His goodness. In addition to this, I discovered the whereabouts of the freshwater pump, and having fixed it, I found the water drinkable, though somewhat unpleasant to the taste.

"For several days, we stayed aboard the ship, without attempting to get to the shore. We were busily engaged in making the place habitable. Yet even thus early, we became aware that our lot was even less to be desired than might have been imagined; for though, as a first step, we scraped away the odd patches of growth that studded the floors and walls of the cabins and saloon, yet they returned almost to their original size within the space of twenty-four hours, which not only discouraged us, but gave us a feeling of vague unease.

"Still, we would not admit ourselves beaten, so set to work afresh, and not only scraped away the fungus, but soaked the places where it had been, with carbolic, a can-full of which I had found in the pantry. Yet, by the end of the week, the growth had returned in full strength, and, in addition, it had spread to other places, as though our touching it had allowed germs from it to travel elsewhere.

"On the seventh morning, my sweetheart woke to find a small patch of it growing on her pillow, close to her face. At that, she came to me, so soon as she could get her garments upon her. I was in the galley at the time, lighting the fire for breakfast.

"'Come here, John,' she said, and led me aft. When I saw the thing upon her pillow, I shuddered, and then and there we agreed to go right out of the ship, and see whether we could not fare to make ourselves more comfortable ashore.

"Hurriedly, we gathered together our few belongings, and even among these, I found that the fungus had been at work; for one of her shawls had a little lump of it growing near one edge. I threw the whole thing over the side, without saying anything to her.

"The raft was still alongside; but it was too clumsy to guide, and I lowered down a small boat that hung across the stern, and in this we made our way to the shore. Yet, as we drew near to it, I became gradually aware that here the vile fungus, which had driven us from the ship, was growing riot. In places it rose into horrible, fantastic mounds, which seemed almost to quiver, as with a quiet life, when the wind blew across them. Here and there, it took on the forms of vast fingers, and in others it just spread out flat and smooth and treacherous. Odd places, it appeared as grotesque stunted trees, seeming extraordinarily kinked and gnarled— The whole quaking vilely at times.

"At first, it seemed to us that there was no single portion of the surrounding shore which was not hidden beneath the masses of the hideous lichen; yet, in this, I found we were mistaken; for somewhat later, coasting along the shore at a little distance, we descried a smooth white patch of what appeared to be fine sand, and there we landed. It was not sand. What it was, I do not know. All that I have observed, is that upon it, the fungus will not grow; while everywhere else, save where the sand-like earth wanders oddly, path-wise, amid the grey desolation of the lichen, there is nothing but that loathsome greyness.

"It is difficult to make you understand how cheered we were to find one place that was absolutely free from the growth, and here we deposited our belongings. Then we went back to the ship for such things as it seemed to us we should need. Among other matters, I managed to bring ashore with me one of the ship's sails, with which I constructed two small tents, which, though exceedingly rough-shaped, served the purposes for which they were intended. In these, we lived and stored our various necessities, and thus for a matter of some four weeks, all went smoothly and without particular unhappiness. Indeed, I may say with much of happiness—for—for we were together.

"It was on the thumb of her right hand, that the growth first showed. It was only a small circular spot, much like a little grey mole. My God! how the fear leapt to my heart when she showed me the place. We cleansed it, between us, washing it with carbolic and water. In the morning of the following day, she showed her hand to me again. The grey warty thing had returned. For a little while, we looked at one another in silence. Then, still wordless, we started again to remove it. In the midst of the operation, she spoke suddenly.

"'What's that on the side of your face, Dear!' Her voice was sharp with anxiety. I put my hand up to feel.

"'There! Under the hair by your ear.—A little to the front a bit.' My finger rested upon the place, and then I knew.

"'Let us get your thumb done first,' I said. And she submitted, only because she was afraid to touch me until it was cleansed. I finished washing and disinfecting her thumb, and then she turned to my face. After it was finished, we sat together and talked awhile of many things; for there had come into our lives sudden, very terrible thoughts. We were, all at once, afraid of something worse than death.We spoke of loading the boat with provisions and water, and making our way out on to the sea; yet we were helpless, for many causes, and—and the growth had attacked us already. We decided to stay. God would do with us what was His will. We would wait.

"A month, two months, three months passed, and the places grew somewhat, and there had come others. Yet we fought so strenuously with the fear, that its headway was but slow, comparatively speaking.

"Occasionally, we ventured off to the ship for such stores as we needed. There, we found that the fungus grew persistently. One of the nodules on the maindeck became soon as high as my head.

"We had now given up all thought or hope of leaving the island. We had realised that it would be unallowable to go among healthy humans, with the thing from which we were suffering.

"With this determination and knowledge in our minds, we knew that we should have to husband our food and water; for we did not know, at that time, but that we should possibly live for many years.

"This reminds me that I have told you that I am an old man. Judged by years this is not so. But—but—"

He broke off; then continued somewhat abruptly:

"As I was saying, we knew that we should have to use care in the matter of food. But we had no idea then how little food there was left, of which to take care. It was a week later, that I made the discovery that all the other bread tanks—which I had supposed full—were empty, and that (beyond odd tins of vegetables and meat, and some other matters) we had nothing on which to depend, but the bread in the tank which I had already opened.

"After learning this, I bestirred myself to do what I could, and set to work at fishing in the lagoon; but with no success. At this, I was somewhat inclined to feel desperate, until the thought came to me to try outside the lagoon, in the open sea.

"Here, at times, I caught odd fish; but, so infrequently, that they proved of but little help in keeping us from the hunger which threatened. It seemed to me that our deaths were likely to come by hunger, and not by the growth of the thing which had seized upon our bodies.

"We were in this state of mind when the fourth month wore out. Then I made a very horrible discovery. One morning, a little before midday, I came off from the ship, with a portion of the biscuits which were left. In the mouth of her tent, I saw my sweetheart sitting, eating something.

"'What is it, my Dear?' I called out as I leapt ashore. Yet, on hearing my voice, she seemed confused, and, turning, slyly threw something towards the edge of the little clearing. It fell short, and, a vague suspicion having arisen within me, I walked across and picked it up. It was a piece of the grey fungus.

"As I went to her, with it in my hand, she turned deadly pale; then a rose red.

"I felt strangely dazed and frightened.

"'My Dear! My Dear!' I said, and could say no more. Yet, at my words, she broke down and cried bitterly. Gradually, as she calmed, I got from her the news that she had tried it the preceding day, and—and liked it. I got her to promise on her knees not to touch it again, however great our hunger. After she had promised, she told me that the desire for it had come suddenly, and that, until the moment of desire, she had experienced nothing towards it, but the most extreme repulsion.

"Later in the day, feeling strangely restless, and much shaken with the thing which I had discovered, I made my way along one of the twisted paths—formed by the white, sand-like substance—which

44

led among the fungoid growth. I had, once before, ventured along there; but not to any great distance. This time, being involved in perplexing thought, I went much further than hitherto.

"Suddenly, I was called to myself, by a queer hoarse sound on my left. Turning quickly, I saw that there was movement among an extraordinarily shaped mass of fungus, close to my elbow. It was swaying uneasily, as though it possessed life of its own. Abruptly, as I stared, the thought came to me that the thing had a grotesque resemblance to the figure of a distorted human creature. Even as the fancy flashed into my brain, there was a slight, sickening noise of tearing, and I saw that one of the branch-like arms was detaching itself from the surrounding grey masses, and coming towards me. The head of the thing—a shapeless grey ball, inclined in my direction. I stood stupidly, and the vile arm brushed across my face. I gave out a frightened cry, and ran back a few paces. There was a sweetish taste upon my lips, where the thing had touched me. I licked them, and was immediately filled with an inhuman desire. I turned and seized a mass of the fungus. Then more, and—more. I was insatiable. In the midst of devouring, the remembrance of the morning's discovery swept into my mazed brain. It was sent by God. I dashed the fragment I held, to the ground. Then, utterly wretched and feeling a dreadful guiltiness, I made my way back to the little encampment.

"I think she knew, by some marvellous intuition which love must have given, so soon as she set eyes on me. Her quiet sympathy made it easier for me, and I told her of my sudden weakness; yet omitted to mention the extraordinary thing which had gone before. I desired to spare her all unnecessary terror.

"But, for myself, I had added an intolerable knowledge, to breed an incessant terror in my brain; for I doubted not but that I had

45

seen the end of one of those men who had come to the island in the ship in the lagoon; and in that monstrous ending, I had seen our own.

"Thereafter, we kept from the abominable food, though the desire for it had entered into our blood. Yet, our drear punishment was upon us; for, day by day, with monstrous rapidity, the fungoid growth took hold of our poor bodies. Nothing we could do would check it materially, and so—and so—we who had been human, became— Well, it matters less each day. Only—only we had been man and maid!

"And day by day, the fight is more dreadful, to withstand the hunger-lust for the terrible lichen.

"A week ago we ate the last of the biscuit, and since that time I have caught three fish. I was out here fishing tonight, when your schooner drifted upon me out of the mist. I hailed you. You know the rest, and may God, out of His great heart, bless you for your goodness to a—a couple of poor outcast souls."

There was the dip of an oar—another. Then the voice came again, and for the last time, sounding through the slight surrounding mist, ghostly and mournful.

"God bless you! Good-bye!"

"Good-bye," we shouted together, hoarsely, our hearts full of many emotions.

I glanced about me. I became aware that the dawn was upon us.

The sun flung a stray beam across the hidden sea; pierced the mist dully, and lit up the receding boat with a gloomy fire. Indistinctly, I saw something nodding between the oars. I thought of a sponge—a great, grey nodding sponge— The oars continued to ply. They were grey—as was the boat—and my eyes searched a moment vainly for the conjunction of hand and oar. My gaze flashed back to the—head. It nodded forward as the oars went backward for the stroke. Then the oars were dipped, the boat shot out of the patch of light, and the—the thing went nodding into the mist.

CATERPILLARS

E. F. Benson

Edward Frederic Benson (1867–1940) was the fifth of six children. His parents were Edward Benson, headmaster of Wellington College, later Archbishop of Canterbury, and Mary (Minnie) Sidgwick. Minnie, younger sister of the moral philosopher, Henry Sidgwick, was described by the Prime Minister, William Gladstone as "the cleverest woman in Europe". Her talented children inherited her intelligence, as well as her defiance of heterosexual constraints. Benson was educated at Marlborough and Kings College Cambridge where he became a member of the Chit-Chat club at which M. R. James would read ghostly stories by candlelight. In the wake of the trials of Oscar Wilde, he shared a villa in Capri with the aesthete, John Ellingham Brooks. Benson was a prolific and versatile writer in multiple genres including biography, the atmospheric ghost story, humorous novel, children's literature, and skating short story. He was an athletic man and represented England at figure skating.

Benson is most widely known for the lightly satiric "Mapp and Lucia" series, in which the esoteric character of Emmeline (Lucia) Mapp is said to be a spoof of the top-selling novelist Marie Corelli. "Caterpillars" comes earlier in his writing career and was published in *The Room in the Tower and Other Stories* (1912) by Mills & Boon before the firm began specializing in romance fiction. It clearly takes inspiration from Benson's time on Capri as it is a first-person narrative of an encounter with supernatural insects occupying an

E. F. BENSON

Italian villa like an infestation. These crab-footed, large and faintly luminous caterpillars are unusual in our anthology in being insects still in their larval stage. Unnerving as they are as a host of crawling grubs, a further part of their menace consists in what they may metamorphose into.

50

saw a month or two ago in an Italian paper that the Villa Cascana, in which I once stayed, had been pulled down, and that a manufactory of some sort was in process of erection on its site. There is therefore no longer any reason for refraining from writing of those things which I myself saw (or imagined I saw) in a certain room and on a certain landing of the villa in question, nor from mentioning the circumstances which followed, which may or may not (according to the opinion of the reader) throw some light on or be somehow connected with this experience.

The Villa Cascana was in all ways but one a perfectly delightful house, yet, if it were standing now, nothing in the world—I use the phrase in its literal sense—would induce me to set foot in it again, for I believe it to have been haunted in a very terrible and practical manner. Most ghosts, when all is said and done, do not do much harm; they may perhaps terrify, but the person whom they visit usually gets over their visitation. They may on the other hand be entirely friendly and beneficent. But the appearances in the Villa Cascana were not beneficent, and had they made their "visit" in a very slightly different manner, I do not suppose I should have got over it any more than Arthur Inglis did.

The house stood on an ilex-clad hill not far from Sestri di Levante on the Italian Riviera, looking out over the iridescent blues of that enchanted sea, while behind it rose the pale green chestnut woods that climb up the hillsides till they give place to the pines that, black in contrast with them, crown the slopes. All round it the garden in the luxuriance of mid-spring bloomed and was fragrant, and the scent of magnolia and rose, borne on the salt freshness of the winds from the sea, flowed like a stream through the cool vaulted rooms.

On the ground floor a broad pillared *loggia* ran round three sides of the house, the top of which formed a balcony for certain rooms of the first floor. The main staircase, broad and of grey marble steps, led up from the hall to the landing outside these rooms, which were three in number, namely two big sitting-rooms and a bedroom arranged *en suite*. The latter was unoccupied, the sitting-rooms were in use. From these the main staircase was continued to the second floor, where were situated certain bedrooms, one of which I occupied, while from the other side of the first-floor landing some half-dozen steps led to another suite of rooms, where, at the time I am speaking of, Arthur Inglis, the artist, had his bedroom and studio. Thus the landing outside my bedroom at the top of the house, commanded both the landing of the first floor, and also the steps that led to Inglis' rooms. Jim Stanley and his wife, finally (whose guest I was), occupied rooms in another wing of the house, where also were the servants' quarters.

I arrived just in time for lunch on a brilliant noon of mid-May. The garden was shouting with colour and fragrance, and not less delightful after my broiling walk up from the *marina*, should have been the coming from the reverberating heat and blaze of the day into the marble coolness of the villa. Only (the reader has my bare word for this, and nothing more), the moment I set foot in the house I felt that something was wrong. This feeling, I may say, was quite vague, though very strong, and I remember that when I saw letters waiting for me on the table in the hall I felt certain that the explanation was here: I was convinced that there was bad news of some sort for me. Yet when I opened them I found no such explanation of my premonition: my correspondents all reeked of prosperity. Yet this clear miscarriage of a presentiment did not dissipate my uneasiness. In that cool fragrant house there was something wrong.

I am at pains to mention this because to the general view it may explain that though I am as a rule so excellent a sleeper that the extinction of my light on getting into bed is apparently contemporaneous with being called on the following morning, I slept very badly on my first night in the Villa Cascana. It may also explain the fact that when I did sleep (if it was indeed in sleep that I saw what I thought I saw) I dreamed in a very vivid and original manner, original, that is to say, in the sense that something that, as far as I knew, had never previously entered into my consciousness, usurped it then. But since, in addition to this evil premonition, certain words and events occurring during the rest of the day, might have suggested something of what I thought happened that night, it will be well to relate them.

After lunch, then, I went round the house with Mrs Stanley, and during our tour she referred, it is true, to the unoccupied bedroom on the first floor, which opened out of the room where we had lunched.

"We left that unoccupied," she said, "because Jim and I have a charming bedroom and dressing-room, as you saw, in the wing, and if we used it ourselves we should have to turn the dining-room into a dressing-room and have our meals downstairs. As it is, however, we have our little flat there, Arthur Inglis has his little flat in the other passage; and I remembered (aren't I extraordinary?) that you once said that the higher up you were in a house the better you were pleased. So I put you at the top of the house, instead of giving you that room."

It is true, that a doubt, vague as my uneasy premonition, crossed my mind at this. I did not see why Mrs Stanley should have explained all this, if there had not been more to explain. I allow, therefore, that the thought that there was something to explain about the unoccupied bedroom was momentarily present to my mind.

The second thing that may have borne on my dream was this.

At dinner the conversation turned for a moment on ghosts. Inglis, with the certainty of conviction, expressed his belief that anybody who could possibly believe in the existence of supernatural phenomena was unworthy of the name of an ass. The subject instantly dropped. As far as I can recollect, nothing else occurred or was said that could bear on what follows.

We all went to bed rather early, and personally I yawned my way upstairs, feeling hideously sleepy. My room was rather hot, and I threw all the windows wide, and from without poured in the white light of the moon, and the love-song of many nightingales. I undressed quickly, and got into bed, but though I had felt so sleepy before, I now felt extremely wide-awake. But I was quite content to be awake: I did not toss or turn, I felt perfectly happy listening to the song and seeing the light. Then, it is possible, I may have gone to sleep, and what follows may have been a dream. I thought anyhow that after a time the nightingales ceased singing and the moon sank. I thought also that if, for some unexplained reason, I was going to lie awake all night, I might as well read, and I remembered that I had left a book in which I was interested in the dining-room on the first floor. So I got out of bed, lit a candle, and went downstairs. I went into the room, saw on a side-table the book I had come to look for, and then, simultaneously, saw that the door into the unoccupied bedroom was open. A curious grey light, not of dawn nor of moonshine, came out of it, and I looked in. The bed stood just opposite the door, a big four-poster, hung with tapestry at the head. Then I saw that the greyish light of the bedroom came from the bed, or rather from what was on the bed. For it was covered with great caterpillars, a foot or more in length, which crawled over it. They were faintly luminous, and it was the light from them that showed me the room. Instead of the sucker-feet of ordinary caterpillars they had rows of pincers like crabs, and they moved by grasping what they lay on with their pincers, and then sliding their bodies forward. In colour these dreadful insects were yellowish-grey, and they were covered with irregular lumps and swellings. There must have been hundreds of them, for they formed a sort of writhing, crawling pyramid on the bed. Occasionally one fell off on to the floor, with a soft fleshy thud, and though the floor was of hard concrete, it yielded to the pincer-feet as if it had been putty, and, crawling back, the caterpillar would mount on to the bed again, to rejoin its fearful companions. They appeared to have no faces, so to speak, but at one end of them there was a mouth that opened sideways in respiration.

Then, as I looked, it seemed to me as if they all suddenly became conscious of my presence. All the mouths at any rate were turned in my direction, and next moment they began dropping off the bed with those soft fleshy thuds on to the floor, and wriggling towards me. For one second a paralysis as of a dream was on me, but the next I was running upstairs again to my room, and I remember feeling the cold of the marble steps on my bare feet. I rushed into my bedroom, and slammed the door behind me, and then—I was certainly wide awake now—I found myself standing by my bed with the sweat of terror pouring from me. The noise of the banged door still rang in my ears. But, as would have been more usual, if this had been mere nightmare, the terror that had been mine when I saw those foul beasts crawling about the bed or dropping softly on to the floor did not cease then. Awake now, if dreaming before, I did not at all recover from the horror of dream: it did not seem to me that I had dreamed. And until dawn, I sat or stood, not daring to lie down, thinking that every rustle or movement that I heard was the approach of the caterpillars. To them and the claws that bit into the cement the wood of the door was child's play: steel would not keep them out.

But with the sweet and noble return of day the horror vanished: the whisper of wind became benignant again: the nameless fear, whatever it was, was smoothed out and terrified me no longer. Dawn broke, hueless at first; then it grew dove-coloured, then the flaming pageant of light spread over the sky.

The admirable rule of the house was that everybody had breakfast where and when he pleased, and in consequence it was not till lunch-time that I met any of the other members of our party, since I had breakfast on my balcony, and wrote letters and other things till lunch. In fact, I got down to that meal rather late, after the other three had begun. Between my knife and fork there was a small pill-box of cardboard, and as I sat down Inglis spoke.

"Do look at that," he said, "since you are interested in natural history. I found it crawling on my counterpane last night, and I don't know what it is."

I think that before I opened the pill-box I expected something of the sort which I found in it. Inside it, anyhow, was a small caterpillar, greyish-yellow in colour, with curious bumps and excrescences on its rings. It was extremely active, and hurried round the box, this way and that. Its feet were unlike the feet of any caterpillar I ever saw: they were like the pincers of a crab. I looked, and shut the lid down again.

"No, I don't know it," I said, "but it looks rather unwholesome. What are you going to do with it?"

"Oh, I shall keep it," said Inglis. "It has begun to spin: I want to see what sort of a moth it turns into."

I opened the box again, and saw that these hurrying movements were indeed the beginning of the spinning of the web of its cocoon. Then Inglis spoke again.

"It has got funny feet, too," he said. "They are like crabs' pincers. What's the Latin for crab? Oh, yes, Cancer. So in case it is unique, let's christen it: 'Cancer Inglisensis.'"

Then something happened in my brain, some momentary piecing together of all that I had seen or dreamed. Something in his words seemed to me to throw light on it all, and my own intense horror at the experience of the night before linked itself on to what he had just said. In effect, I took the box and threw it, caterpillar and all, out of the window. There was a gravel path just outside, and beyond it, a fountain playing into a basin. The box fell on to the middle of this.

Inglis laughed.

"So the students of the occult don't like solid facts," he said. "My poor caterpillar!"

The talk went off again at once on to other subjects, and I have only given in detail, as they happened, these trivialities in order to be sure myself that I have recorded everything that could have borne on occult subjects or on the subject of caterpillars. But at the moment when I threw the pill-box into the fountain, I lost my head: my only excuse is that, as is probably plain, the tenant of it was, in miniature, exactly what I had seen crowded on to the bed in the unoccupied room. And though this translation of those phantoms into flesh and blood—or whatever it is that caterpillars are made of—ought perhaps to have relieved the horror of the night, as a matter of fact it did nothing of the kind. It only made the crawling pyramid that covered the bed in the unoccupied room more hideously real.

After lunch we spent a lazy hour or two strolling about the garden or sitting in the loggia, and it must have been about four o'clock when Stanley and I started off to bathe, down the path that led by the fountain into which I had thrown the pill-box. The water was shallow and clear, and at the bottom of it I saw its white remains. The water had disintegrated the cardboard, and it had become no more than a few strips and shreds of sodden paper. The centre of the fountain was a marble Italian Cupid which squirted the water out of a wine-skin held under its arm. And crawling up its leg was the caterpillar. Strange and scarcely credible as it seemed, it must have survived the falling-to-bits of its prison, and made its way to shore, and there it was, out of arm's reach, weaving and waving this way and that as it evolved its cocoon.

Then, as I looked at it, it seemed to me again that, like the caterpillar I had seen last night, it saw me, and breaking out of the threads that surrounded it, it crawled down the marble leg of the Cupid and began swimming like a snake across the water of the fountain towards me. It came with extraordinary speed (the fact of a caterpillar being able to swim was new to me), and in another moment was crawling up the marble lip of the basin. Just then Inglis joined us.

"Why, if it isn't old 'Cancer Inglisensis' again," he said, catching sight of the beast. "What a tearing hurry it is in."

We were standing side by side on the path, and when the caterpillar had advanced to within about a yard of us, it stopped, and began waving again, as if in doubt as to the direction in which it should go. Then it appeared to make up its mind, and crawled on to Inglis' shoe.

"It likes me best," he said, "but I don't really know that I like it. And as it won't drown I think perhaps—"

He shook it off his shoe on to the gravel path and trod on it.

All afternoon the air got heavier and heavier with the Sirocco that was without doubt coming up from the south, and that night again I went up to bed feeling very sleepy; but below my drowsiness, so to speak, there was the consciousness, stronger than before, that there was something wrong in the house, that something dangerous was close at hand. But I fell asleep at once, and—how long after I do not know—either woke or dreamed I awoke, feeling that I must get up at once, *or I should be too late*. Then (dreaming or awake) I lay and fought this fear, telling myself that I was but the prey of my own nerves disordered by Sirocco or what not, and at the same time quite clearly knowing in another part of my mind, so to speak, that every moment's delay added to the danger. At last this second feeling became irresistible, and I put on coat and trousers and went out of my room on to the landing. And then I saw that I had already delayed too long, and that I was now too late.

The whole of the landing of the first floor below was invisible under the swarm of caterpillars that crawled there. The folding doors into the sitting-room from which opened the bedroom where I had seen them last night, were shut, but they were squeezing through the cracks of it, and dropping one by one through the keyhole, elongating themselves into mere string as they passed, and growing fat and lumpy again on emerging. Some, as if exploring, were nosing about the steps into the passage at the end of which were Inglis' rooms, others were crawling on the lowest steps of the staircase that led up to where I stood. The landing, however, was completely covered with them: I was cut off. And of the frozen horror that seized me when I saw that, I can give no idea in words.

Then at last a general movement began to take place, and they grew thicker on the steps that led to Inglis' room. Gradually, like some hideous tide of flesh, they advanced along the passage, and I saw the foremost, visible by the pale grey luminousness that came from them, reach his door. Again and again I tried to shout and warn him, in terror all the time that they would turn at the sound of my voice and mount my stair instead, but for all my efforts I felt that no sound came from my throat. They crawled along the hinge-crack of his door, passing through as they had done before, and still I stood there making impotent efforts to shout to him, to bid him escape while there was time.

At last the passage was completely empty: they had all gone, and at that moment I was conscious for the first time of the cold of the marble landing on which I stood barefooted. The dawn was just beginning to break in the Eastern sky.

Six months later I met Mrs Stanley in a country house in England. We talked on many subjects and at last she said:

"I don't think I have seen you since I got that dreadful news about Arthur Inglis a month ago."

"I haven't heard," said I.

"No? He has got cancer. They don't even advise an operation, for there is no hope of a cure: he is riddled with it, the doctors say."

Now during all these six months I do not think a day had passed on which I had not had in my mind the dreams (or whatever you like to call them) which I had seen in the Villa Cascana.

"It is awful, is it not?" she continued, "and I feel, I can't help feeling, that he may have—"

"Caught it at the villa?" I asked.

She looked at me in blank surprise.

"Why did you say that?" she asked. "How did you know?"

Then she told me. In the unoccupied bedroom a year before there had been a fatal case of cancer. She had, of course, taken the best advice and had been told that the utmost dictates of prudence would be obeyed so long as she did not put anybody to sleep in the room, which had also been thoroughly disinfected and newly white-washed and painted. But—

CELUI-LÀ

Eleanor Scott

Eleanor Scott (1892–1965) was the penname for Helen Leys, an Oxford educated teacher who tried her hand at writing ghost stories during the boom of the genre in the late 1920s. Her first haunted-chamber tales "The Room", originally published in the *Cornhill Magazine* in 1923, appeared under her own name. It was only after writing the controversial novel *War Among Ladies*, which formed a scathing indictment of the English girls' high school system, that the pseudonym "Eleanor Scott" was born.

Under this name she would publish a total of five novels, none of them speculative, and a pair of collective biographies for children. It is now believed that Leys also wrote a pair of non-supernatural mystery novels under the pseudonym "P. R. Shore".

In 2012, "Celui-Là" was selected by John Pelan to represent the year 1929 in his two-volume anthology *The Century's Best Horror Fiction*. Scott points to her dreams as her primary source of inspiration, but one wonders how much these were influenced by the work she read. There is no denying the influence of M. R. James on her work, specifically on "The Twelve Apostles" and "Celui-Là", with the latter seeming to blend aspects of multiple tales: "The Treasure of Abbot Thomas", "Oh, Whistle, and I'll Come to You, My Lad" and "Count Magnus".

don't for a moment expect you to take my advice," said Dr. Foster, looking shrewdly at his patient, "but I'll give it all the same. It's this. Pack a bag with a few things and go off to-morrow to some tiny seaside or mountain place, preferably out of England, so that you won't meet a soul you know. Live there absolutely quietly for three or four weeks, taking a reasonable amount of exercise, and then write and tell me that you're all right again."

"Easier said than done," growled Maddox. "There aren't any quiet places left that I know of, and if there were there wouldn't be any digs to be had at no notice."

Foster considered.

"I know the very thing," he cried suddenly. "There's a little place on the Breton coast—fishing village, very small and scattered, with a long stretch of beach, heath and moor inland, quiet as can be. I happen to know the curé there quite fairly well, and he's an extremely decent, homely little chap. Vétier his name is. He'd take you in. I'll write to him to-night."

After that, Maddox couldn't in decency hold out. Old Foster had been very good, really, over the whole thing; besides, it was nearly as much bother to fight him as it was to go. In less than a week Maddox was on his way to Kerouac.

Foster saw him off with relief. He knew Maddox well, and knew that he was suffering from years of overwork and worry; he understood how very repugnant effort of any kind was to him—or thought he did; but in reality no one can quite understand the state of exasperation or depression that illness can produce in someone else. Yet as the absurd little train that Maddox took at Lamballe puffed serenely along between tiny rough orchards, the overwrought passenger began to feel soothed; and then, as the line turned north and west, and the cool wind came in from across the dim stretches of moorland, he grew content and almost serene.

Dusk had fallen when he got out at the shed that marked the station of Kerouac. The curé, a short, plump man, in soutane and broad-brimmed hat, met him with the kind, almost effusive, greeting that Breton peasants give to a guest, and conducted the stumbling steps of his visitor to a rough country lane falling steeply downhill between two high, dark banks that smelt of gorse and heather and damp earth. Maddox could just see the level line of sea lying before him, framed by the steep banks of moor on either hand. Above a few pale stars glimmered in the dim sky. It was very peaceful.

Maddox fell into the simple life of the Kerouac presbytery at once. The curé was, as Foster had said, a very homely, friendly little man, always serene and nearly always busy, for he had a large and scattered flock and took a very real interest in the affairs of each member of it. Also, Maddox gathered, money was none too plentiful, for the curé did all the work of the church himself, even down to the trimming of the grass and shrubs that surrounded the little wind-swept building.

The country also appealed very strongly to the visitor. It was at once desolate and friendly, rough and peaceful. He particularly liked the long reaches of the shore, where the tangle of heath and whin gave place to tufts of coarse, whitish grass and then to a belt of shingle and the long level stretches of smooth sand. He liked to walk there when evening had fallen, the moorland on his left rising black to the grey sky, the sea, smooth and calm, stretching out infinitely on his right, a shining ripple lifting here and there. Oddly enough, M. le Curé did not seem to approve of these evening rambles; but that, Maddox told himself, was common among peasants of all races; and he idly wondered whether this were due to a natural liking for the fireside after a day in the open, or whether there were in it some ancient fear of the spirits and demons that country people used to fear in the dim time *entre le chien et le loup.* Anyhow, he wasn't going to give up his evening strolls for a superstition of someone else's!

It was near the end of October, but very calm weather for the time of year; and one evening the air was so mild and the faint shine of the stars so lovely that Maddox extended his walk beyond its usual limits. He had always had the beach to himself at that time of the evening; and he felt a natural, if quite unjustifiable, annoyance when he first noticed that there was someone else on the shore.

The figure was perhaps fifty yards away. At first he thought it was a peasant woman, for it had some sort of hood drawn over the head, and the arms, which it was waving or wringing, were covered by long, hanging sleeves. Then, as he drew nearer, he saw that it was far too tall for a woman, and jumped to the conclusion that it must be a monk or wandering friar of quite exceptional height.

The light was very dim, for the new moon had set, and the stars showed a faint diffused light among thin drifts of cloud; but even so Maddox could not help noticing that the person before him was behaving very oddly. It—he could not determine the sex—moved at an incredible speed up and down a short stretch of beach, waving its draped arms; then suddenly, to his horror, it broke out into a hideous cry, like the howl of a dog. There was something in that cry that turned Maddox cold. Again it rose, and again—an eerie, wailing, hooting sound, dying away over the empty moor. And then the creature dropped on its knees and began scratching at the sand with its hands. A memory, forgotten until now, flashed into Maddox's mind—a memory of that rather horrible story in Hans Andersen about Anne Lisbeth and the drowned child...

The thin cloud obscured the faint light for a moment. When Maddox looked again the figure was still crouching on the shore, scrabbling with its fingers in the loose sand; and this time it gave Maddox the impression of something else—a horrible impression of an enormous toad. He hesitated, and then swallowing down his reluctance with an effort, walked towards the crouching, shrouded figure.

As he approached it suddenly sprang upright, and with a curious, gliding movement, impossible to describe, sped away inland at an incredible speed, its gown flapping as it went. Again Maddox heard the longdrawn mournful howl.

Maddox stood gazing through the thickening dusk.

"Of course it's impossible to tell in this light," he muttered to himself, "but it certainly did look extraordinarily tall—and what an odd look it had of being *flat*. It looked like a scarecrow, with no thickness..."

He wondered at his own relief that the creature had gone. He told himself that it was because he loathed any abnormality, and there could be no doubt that the person he had seen, whether it were woman or monk, was crazed, if not quite insane.

He walked to the place where it had crouched. Yes, there was the patch of disturbed sand, rough among the surrounding smoothness. It occurred to him to look for the footprints made by the flying figure to see if they bore out his impression of abnormal height; but either the light was too bad for him to find them, or the creature

68

had leapt straight on to the belt of shingle. At any rate, there were no footmarks visible.

Maddox knelt beside the patch of disturbed sand and half idly, half in interest, began himself to sift it through his fingers. He felt something hard and smooth—a stone perhaps? He took it up.

It was not a stone, anyhow, though the loose, damp sand clung to it so that he could not clearly distinguish what it was. He got to his feet, clearing it with his handkerchief; and then he saw that it was a box or case, three or four inches long, covered with some kind of rude carving. It fell open of itself as he turned it about, and he saw that inside was a wrapping of something like, yet unlike, leather; inside again was something that crackled like paper.

He looked round to see whether the figure that had either buried or sought this object—he was not sure which it had done—was returning; but he could see nothing but the bushes of gorse and heath black and stunted against the grey sky. There was no sound but the sigh of the night wind and the gentle lap of the incoming tide. His curiosity proved too strong for him, and he slipped the case into his pocket as he turned homewards.

Supper—a simple meal of soup and cheese and cider—was awaiting him when he got in, and he had no time to do more than change his shoes and wash his hands; but after supper, sitting on one side of the wide hearth while the curé smoked placidly on the other, Maddox felt the little box in his pocket, and began to tell his host of his queer adventure.

The curé's lack of enthusiasm rather damped him. No, he knew of no woman in the whole of his wide parish who would behave as Maddox described. There was no monastery in the neighbourhood, and if there were it would not be permitted to the brethren to act like that. He seemed mildly incredulous, in fact, until Maddox, quite nettled, took out the little case and slapped it down on the table.

It was a more uncommon object than he had at first supposed. It was, to begin with, extremely heavy and hard—as heavy as lead, but of a far harder metal. The chasing was queer; the figures reminded Maddox of runes; and remembering the prehistoric remains in Brittany, a thrill ran through him. He was no antiquarian, but it occurred to him that this find of his might be an extremely interesting one.

He opened the case. As he had thought, there was a scrap of some leathery substance within, carefully rolled round a piece of parchment. That couldn't be prehistoric, of course; but Maddox was still interested. He smoothed it out and began stumblingly to read out the crabbed words. The language was Latin of a sort, and he was so occupied in endeavouring to make out the individual words that he made no attempt to construe their meaning until Father Vétier stopped him with a horrified cry and even tried to snatch the document out of his hand.

Maddox looked up, exceedingly startled. The little priest was quite pale, and looked as horrified as if he had been asked to listen to the most shocking blasphemy.

"Why, *mon père*, what's wrong?" asked Maddox, astonished.

"You should not read things like that," panted the little curé. "It is wrong to have that paper. It is a great sin."

"Why? What does it mean? I wasn't translating."

A little colour crept back to the priest's cheeks, but he still looked greatly disturbed.

"It was an invocation," he whispered, glancing over his shoulder. "It is a terrible paper, that. It calls up—*that one*."

Maddox's eyes grew bright and eager.

"Not really? Is it, honestly?" He opened out the sheet again.

The priest sprang to his feet.

"No, Monsieur, I must beg you! No! You have not understood—"

He looked so agitated that Maddox felt compunction. After all, the little chap had been very decent to him, and if he took it like that—! But he couldn't help thinking that it was a pity to let these ignorant peasants have jobs as parish priests. Really, there was enough superstition in their church as it was without drafting old forgotten country charms and incantations into it. A little annoyed, he put the paper back into its case and dropped the whole thing into his pocket. He knew quite well that if the curé got his hands on it he would have no scruples whatever about destroying the whole thing.

That evening did not pass as pleasantly as usual. Maddox felt irritated by the crass ignorance of his companion, and Father Vétier was quite unlike his customary placid self. He seemed nervous, timid even; and Maddox noticed that when the presbytery cat sprang on to the back of her master's chair and rubbed her head silently against his ear the curé almost sprang out of his seat as he hurriedly crossed himself. The time dragged until Maddox could propose retiring to bed; and long after he had been in his room he could hear Father Vétier (for the inner walls of the presbytery were mere lath and plaster) whispering prayers and clicking the beads of his rosary.

When morning came Maddox felt rather ashamed of himself for having alarmed the little priest, as he undoubtedly had done. His compunction increased when he saw Father Vétier as he came in from his early Mass, for the little man looked quite pale and downcast. Maddox mentally cursed himself. He felt like a man who has distressed a child, and he cast about for some small way of making amends. Halfway through déjeuner he had an idea.

"Father," he said, "you are making alterations in your church here, are you not?"

The little man brightened visibly. This, Maddox knew, was his pet hobby.

"But yes, Monsieur," he replied quite eagerly. "For some time now I have been at work, now that at last I have enough. Monseigneur has given me his blessing. It is, you see, that there is beside our church here the fragment of an old building—oh, but old! One says that perhaps it also was a church or a shrine once, but what do I know?—but it is very well built, very strong, and I conceived the idea that one might join it to the church. Figure to yourself, Monsieur, I should then have a double aisle! It will be magnificent. I shall paint it, naturally, to make all look as it should. The church is already painted of a blue of the most heavenly, for the Holy Virgin, with lilies in white—I had hoped for lilies of gold, but gold paint, it is incredible, the cost!—and the new chapel I will have in crimson for the Sacred Heart, with hearts of yellow as a border. It will be gay, isn't it?"

Maddox shuddered inwardly.

"Very gay," he agreed gloomily. There was something that appealed to him very much in the shabby whitewashed little church. He felt pained at the very thought of Father Vétier's blue and crimson and yellow. But the little curé noticed nothing.

"Already I have begun the present church," he babbled, "and, monsieur, you should see it! It is truly celestial, that colour. Now I shall begin to prepare the old building, so that, as soon as the walls are built to join it to the present church, I can decorate. They will not take long, those little walls, not long at all, and then I shall paint..."

He seemed lost in a vision of rapture. Maddox was both amused and touched. Good little chap, it had been a shame to annoy him over that silly incantation business. He felt a renewed impulse to please the friendly little man.

"Can I help you at all, Father?" he asked. "Could I scrape the walls for you or anything like that? I won't offer to paint; I'm not expert enough."

The priest positively beamed. He was a genial soul who loved company, even at his work; but even more he loved putting on thick layers of bright colours according to his long-planned design. To have a companion who did not wish to paint was more than he had ever hoped for. He accepted with delight.

After breakfast, Maddox was taken to see the proposed addition to the church. It stood on the north side of the little church (which, of course, ran east and west), and, as far as Maddox could see, consisted mainly of a piece of masonry running parallel with the wall of the church. Fragments of walls, now crumbled, almost joined it to the east and west ends of the north wall of the church; it might almost have been, at one time, a part of the little church. It certainly, as Father Vétier had said, would not take much alteration to connect it to the church as a north aisle. Maddox set to work to chip the plaster facing from the old wall with a good will.

In the afternoon the curé announced that he had to pay a visit to a sick man some miles away. He accepted with great gratitude his visitor's proposal that he should continue the preparations for the painting of the new aisle. With such efficient help, he said, he would have the addition to the church ready for the great feast of

St. Michael, patron saint both of the village and the church. Maddox was delighted to see how completely his plan had worked in restoring the little man's placid good-humour.

Shortly after two, Maddox went into the churchyard and resumed his labours. He chipped away industriously, and was just beginning to find the work pall when he made a discovery that set him chipping again eagerly at the coat of plaster which later hands had daubed thickly on the original wall. There were undoubtedly mural paintings on the portion he had begun to uncover. Soon he had laid bare quite a large stretch, and could see that the decoration formed a band, six or seven feet deep, about two feet from the ground, nearly the whole length of the wall.

The light was fading, and the colours were dim, but Maddox could see enough to interest him extremely. The paintings seemed to represent a stretch of the seashore, and though the landscape was treated conventionally he thought it looked like part of the beach near Kerouac. There were figures in the painting, too; and these aroused his excitement, for one at least was familiar. It was a tall shape, hooded, with hanging draperies—the figure he had seen the night before on the beach. Perhaps it was due to the archaic treatment of the picture that this figure gave him the same impression of flatness. The other figure—if it was a figure—was even stranger. It crouched on the ground before the hooded shape, and to Maddox it suggested some rather disgusting animal—a toad or a thick, squat fish. The odd thing was that, although it squatted before the tall figure, it gave the impression of domination.

Maddox felt quite thrilled. He peered closely at the painting, endeavouring to make out clearly what it represented; but the short October afternoon was drawing in fast, and, beyond his first impression, he could gather very little. He noticed that there was one unexpected feature in the otherwise half-familiar landscape—a hillock or pile of large stones or rocks, on one side of which he could just make out words or fragments of words. "*Qui peuct venir*" he read in one place, and, lower down, "*Celuy qui ecoustera et qui viendra... sacri... mmes pendus...*"

There was also some vague object, a pile of seaweed, Maddox thought, lying heaped below the hillock.

Little though he knew either of art or of archaeology, Maddox was keenly interested by this discovery. He felt sure that this queer painting must represent some local legend or superstition. And it was very odd that he should have seen, or thought he had seen, that figure on the beach *before* he had discovered the mural painting. There could be no doubt that he had seen it; that it was no mere fancy of his tired mind there was the box and the incantation, or whatever it was, in his pocket to prove. And that gave him an idea. It would be extremely interesting if he should find that the old French words on the mural painting and the Latin words on the parchment in any way corresponded. He took the little metal case from his pocket and opened it.

'*Clamabo et exaudiet me.*' 'I will call and he will hear.' That might be any prayer. Sounds rather like a psalm. '*Quoniam iste qui venire potest*'—ah! '*qui peuct venir*'!—what's this? *sacrificium hominum*—Heavens! *What's that?*"

Far off across the heath he heard a faint cry—the distant howling of the thing he had seen on the beach...

He listened intently. He could hear nothing more.

"Some dog howling," he said to himself. "I'm getting jumpy. Where was I?"

He turned back to the manuscript; but even during the few moments of distraction the light had faded, and he had to strain his eyes to see anything of the words.

"'*E paludinis ubi est habitaculum tuum ego te convoco*'," he read slowly aloud, spelling out the worn writing. "I don't think there's anything in the painting to correspond with that. How odd it is! 'From the marshes where thy dwelling is I call thee.' Why from the *marshes*, I wonder? '*E paludinis ubi est habitaculum tuum ego te convoco*—'."

He broke off abruptly. Again there came that dreadful howl—and it certainly was not the howl of a dog. It was quite close...

Maddox did not stop to consider. He leapt up, ran through the yard into the presbytery, and locked the door behind him. He went to the front door and locked that too; and he bolted every window in the tiny house. Then, and not till then, did he pause to wonder at his own precipitate flight. He was trembling violently, his breath coming in painful gasps. He told himself that he had acted like a hysterical old maid—like a schoolgirl. And yet he could not bring himself to open a window. He went into the little sitting-room and made up the fire to an unwonted size; then he tried to take an interest in Father Vétier's library of devotional books until the little curé himself should return. He was nervous and uneasy; it seemed to him that he could hear some creature (he told himself that it must be a large dog, or perhaps a goat) snuffling about the walls and under the door... He was inexpressibly relieved when at last he heard the short, decided step of the curé coming up the path to the house.

Maddox was restless that night. He had short, heavy snatches of sleep in which he was haunted by dreams of pursuit by that flat, hooded being; and once he woke with a strangled cry and a cold shudder of disgust from a dream that, in his flight, he had stumbled and fallen face downwards on something soft and cold which moved beneath him—a mass of toads… He lay awake for a long time after that dream; but he eventually slipped into a drowsy state, half waking and half sleeping, in which he had an uncomfortable impression that he was not alone in the room—that something was breathing close beside him, moving about in a fumbling, stealthy way. And his nerves were so overwrought that he simply had not the courage to put out a hand and feel for the matches lest his fingers should close on—something else. He did not try to imagine what.

Towards dawn he fell into an uneasy doze, and awoke with a start. Some sound had awakened him—a melancholy howling cry rang in his ears; but whether it had actually sounded or whether it was part of his memories and evil dreams he could not tell.

He looked ill and worn at breakfast, and gave his bad night as an excuse for failing to continue his work on the old wall. He spent a wretched, moping day; he could settle to nothing indoors.

At last, tempted by the mellow October sun, he decided to go for a brisk, short walk. He would return before dusk—he was quite firm about that—and he would avoid the lonely reaches of the shore.

The afternoon was delicious. The rich scent of the gorse and heather, warm in the sun, and the cool touch from the sea that just freshened the breeze, soothed and calmed Maddox wonderfully. He had almost forgotten his terrors of the night before—at least, he was able to push them into a back corner of his mind. He turned homewards contentedly—even in his new calm he was not going to be out after sundown—when his eyes happened to fall on the white road where the declining sun threw his shadow, long and thin, before him. As he saw that shadow, his heart gave a sudden heavy *thud*; for a second shadow walked beside his own.

He spun round. No mortal creature was in sight. The road stretched empty behind him, and on either hand the moorland spread its breast to the wide sky. He ran to the presbytery like a hunted thing.

That evening Father Vétier ventured to speak to him.

"Monsieur," he said, rather timidly, "I do not wish to intrude myself into your affairs. That understands itself. But I have promised my very good friend M. Foster that I will take care of you. You are not a Catholic, I know; but—will you wear this?"

As he spoke he took from his own neck a thin silver chain to which was attached a little medal, black with age, and held it out to his guest.

"Thank you, father," said Maddox simply, slipping the chain about his neck.

"Ah! That is well," said the little curé with satisfaction. "And now, monsieur, I venture to ask you—will you let me change your room? I have one, not as good as yours, I admit it, but which has in it a small opening into the church. You will perhaps repose yourself better there. You will permit?"

"With the greatest pleasure," said Maddox fervently. "You are very kind to me, father."

The little man patted his hand.

"It is that I like you very much, monsieur," he said naively. "And—I am not altogether a fool. We of Brittany see much that we do not look at, and hear much to which we do not listen."

"Father," said Maddox awkwardly, "I want to ask you something. When I began to read out that paper—you remember?—" (The curé nodded uneasily)—"you said that it was an invocation—that it summoned *celui-là*. Did you mean—the devil?"

"No, my son. I—I cannot tell you. It has no name with us of Kerouac. We say, simply, *celui-là*. You will not, if you please, speak of it again. It is not good to speak of it."

"No, I can imagine it isn't," said Maddox; and the conversation dropped.

Maddox certainly slept better that night. In the morning he told himself that this might be for more than one reason. The bed might be more comfortable (but he knew it was not that); *or* he might have overtired himself the day before; or the little curé's offerings might somehow have given him a kind of impression of safety and protection without really having the least power to guard him. His feeling of security increased when the priest announced:

"To-morrow we have another guest, monsieur. M. Foster has done me the honour to accept my invitation for a visit."

"Foster? Really? Excellent," cried Maddox. He felt that the doctor stood for science and civilisation and sanity and all the comfortable reassuring things of life that were so utterly lacking in the desolate wildness of Kerouac.

Sure enough, Foster came next day, and was just as stolid and ugly and completely reassuring as Maddox had hoped he would be and half feared he would not. He seemed to be ignoring his friend's physical condition at first; but on the day after his arrival he got to business.

"Maddox, I don't know how you expect to get fit again," he said. "You came here for the air as much as anything. I said you were to take moderate exercise. Yet here you stick, moping about this poky little house." (Needless to say, Father Vétier was not present when this conversation took place.) "What's wrong with the place, eh? I'd have said it was excellent walking country."

Maddox flushed a little.

"It's a bit boring, walking alone," he said evasively, well aware that "boring" was not the right word.

"Perhaps... Yes. But you can get out a bit more now I'm here to come along. You might take me out this afternoon; the cure's going off to some kind of conference."

Maddox wondered uneasily how much Foster knew. Had he come by chance, off his own bat? Or had Father Vétier been worried about his first guest and sent for him? If that were so, what exactly had the priest said? He thought he'd soon get that out of Foster.

They walked along the beach, farther than Maddox had yet been. He had avoided the shore of late, and he had not felt up to going so far when he first came to Kerouac; yet, though he knew he had never been on that particular reach of shore, the place seemed familiar. It is, of course, a common thing to feel that one knows a place which one is now seeing for the first time; but the impression was so extremely vivid that Maddox couldn't help remarking on it to his companion.

"Rot, my dear man," said Foster bluntly. "You haven't been in Brittany before, and you say you've never been as far as this. It's not such uncommon country, you know; it's like lots of other places."

"I know," said Maddox; but he was not satisfied.

He was poor company for the rest of the walk, and was very silent on the way home. No amount of chaff from Foster could rouse him, and at last the doctor abandoned the effort. The men reached the presbytery in silence.

The next day was close, threatening rain, though the downpour held off from hour to hour. Neither of the two Englishmen felt inclined to walk under that lowering sky. Father Vétier had a second urgent summons from his sick parishioner at Cap Morel, and set off, wrapped in a curious garment of tarpaulin, soon after the second déjeuner. He remarked that he might take the occasion of being so near to Prénoeuf to pay some visits there, and that he probably would not be in until nightfall.

"If monsieur should feel disposed," he said rather shyly to Maddox before he left, "M. Foster might be interested to see the alterations I propose for the church. He has taste, M. Foster. It might amuse him..."

He was so clearly keen to display his decorations, and yet a little afraid of appearing vain if he showed them himself, that Maddox smiled.

"I'm sure he'd like to see them," he said gently.

Yet, though he could have given no possible reason for it, he felt strongly disinclined to go near that half-ruined wall with its stretch of painting only half displayed. He knew it was absurd. He had worked there till he was tired; he had been startled by the howling of a dog. That was all. No doubt, when he came to look at it again, he would find that the fresco was the merest clumsy daub, and that his own overwrought nerves, together with the uncanny light of the gloaming and the beastly dog, had exaggerated it into something sinister and horrible. He declared to himself that if he had the courage to go and look again, he would simply laugh at himself and his terrors. But at the back of his mind he knew that he would never have gone alone; and it was a mixture of bravado and a kind of hope that Foster's horse-sense would lay his terror for him that finally induced him to propose a visit to the place.

Foster was interested, mildly, by what Maddox told him of the painting on the ruined wall. He went out first to the rough little churchyard; Maddox, half reluctantly, went to fetch down the little case he had picked up on the beach in order that Foster might with his own eyes compare the two inscriptions; and when he did go out to join his friend he could hardly bring himself to go over to the wall he had worked on. It took quite an effort to force his feet over to it.

The decoration was not quite as he had remembered it. The figures were so indistinct and faint that they were hardly visible. In fact, Maddox could well believe that a stranger would not recognise the daub as representing figures at all. His relief at this discovery was quite absurd. He felt as if an immense and crushing weight had been lifted from his spirit; and, his first anxiety over, he bent to examine the rest of the painting more attentively. That was nearly exactly as he remembered it—the pile of stones with the half-illegible words; the tumbled huddle of seaweed or rags lying before it; the long reach of shore—ah! that was it!

"Foster! Come and look here," he said.

"Where?" asked the doctor, strolling over.

"Look—this fresco or whatever it is. I said that bit of shore we saw yesterday was familiar. This is where I saw it."

"Mmmm. Might be... All very much alike, though, this part of the beach. I don't see anything to get worked up about."

"Oh! If you're going to take that line!" cried Maddox, exasperated. "You doctors are all alike—'Keep calm'—'Don't get excited'— 'Nothing to worry about'!..."

He broke off, gulping with sheer rage.

"My dear Maddox!" said Foster, startled by his silent friend's outburst. "I'm awfully sorry. I wasn't trying to snub you in the least. I simply thought—" He too broke off. Then he decided to risk another annoyance. "What have you got on your mind?" he asked, rather urgently. "Tell me, Maddox, there's a good chap. What is it?"

He paused hopefully; but Maddox had dried up. He could not explain. He knew that his solid, comfortable friend would never, *could* never understand that his terror was not imaginary; he could not bear to watch him soothing down his friend, to see the thought "hysteria" in his mind... Yet it would be a relief to tell...

"Look at this," he said at last. He took from his pocket the case he had found on the beach. "What do you make of that paper?" he asked.

Foster moved out of the shadow of the wall so that the pale watery sunlight, struggling through the clouds, fell on the parchment. Maddox, a little relieved by the serious way he took it, turned back to examine the painting again. It was certainly very odd that the figures, which he remembered so clearly and which had seemed so very distinct, should now appear so dim that he doubted their reality. They seemed even fainter now than they had when he had looked at them a few minutes ago. And that heap flung beneath the hillock—what did that represent? He began to wonder whether that, too, were a figure—a drowned man, perhaps. He bent closer, and, as he stooped, he was aware that some one beside him was looking over his shoulder, almost leaning on him.

"Odd, Foster, isn't it?" he said. "What do you make of that huddled thing under the stones?"

There was no answer, and Maddox turned. Then he sprang to his feet with a shuddering cry that died in his throat. The thing so close to him was not his friend. It was the hooded creature of the beach...

Foster found the parchment so interesting that he was anxious to see it more clearly. He peered at it closely for a minute, and then decided to go into the presbytery for a light. He had some difficulty with the old-fashioned oil lamp; but when he finally got it burning he thought that the document fully repaid his trouble. He became so absorbed that it was not for some minutes that he realised that it was growing very dark and that Maddox had not yet come in. He felt quite disproportionately anxious as he hurried out to the tiny overgrown churchyard.

He was startled into something very like panic when he found no one there. Without reason, he knew that there was something horribly wrong, and, blindly obeying the same instinct, he rushed out of the tiny enclosure and ran at his top speed down to the beach. He knew that he would find whatever there was to find on that lonely reach that was pictured on the old wall.

There was a faint glimmer of daylight still—enough to confuse the light until Foster, half distraught with a nameless fear, could hardly tell substance from shadow. But once he thought he saw ahead of him two figures—one a man's, and the other a tall wavering shape almost indistinguishable in the gloom.

The sand dragged at his feet till they felt like lead. He struggled on, his breath coming in gasps that tore his lungs. Then, at last, the sand gave way to coarse grass and then to a stretch of salt marshland, where the mud oozed up over his shoes and water came lapping about his ankles. Open pools lay here and there, and he saw, as he struggled and tore his feet from the viscous slime, horrible creatures like toads or thick, squat fish, moving heavily in the watery ooze.

The light had almost gone as he reached the line of beach he knew: and for one terrible moment he thought he was too late. There was the pile of stones; beneath them lay a huddled black mass. Something—was it a shadow?—wavered, tall and vague, above the heap, and before it squatted a shape that turned Foster cold—something thick, lumpish, like an enormous toad...

He screamed as he dragged his feet from the loathsome mud that clooped and gulped under him—screamed aloud for help...

Then suddenly he heard a voice—a human voice.

"*In nomine Dei Omnipotenti...*" it cried.

Foster made one stupendous effort, and fell forward on his knees. The blood sang in his ears, but through the hammering of his pulses he heard a sound like the howling of a dog dying away in the distance.

"It was by the providence of the good God that I was there," said Father Vétier afterwards. "I do not often come by the shore—we of Kerouac, monsieur, we do not like the shore after it is dusk. But it was late, and the road by the shore is quicker. Indeed I think the good saints led me... But if my fear had been stronger so that I had not gone that way—and it was very strong, monsieur—I do not think that your friend would be living now."

"Nor do I," said Foster soberly. "My God, Father, it—it was nearly over. *Sacrificium hominum*, that beastly paper said... I—I saw the loathsome thing waiting... he was lying in front of that hellish altar or whatever it was... *Why*, Father? Why did it have that power over him?"

"I think it was that he read the—the invocation—aloud," said the curé slowly. "He called it, do you see, monsieur—he said the words. What he saw at first is—is often seen. We are used to it, we of Kerouac. We call it *Celui-là*. But it is, I believe, only a servant of—that other..."

"Well," said Foster soberly, "you're a brave man, Padre. I wouldn't spend an hour here if I could help it. As soon as poor Maddox can travel I'm going home with him. As to living here alone—!"

"And you are right to go," said Father Vétier, gravely. "But for me—no, monsieur. It is my post, do you see. And one prays, monsieur—one prays always."

"HE MADE A WOMAN—"

Marjorie Bowen

Marjorie Bowen is one of the many pseudonyms of Margaret Gabrielle Vere Long (1885–1952), an extraordinarily prolific British writer who published well over a hundred novels, short story collections and works of non-fiction in her various guises. Like Mary Webb, she was an important writer in her time who has now largely fallen into obscurity. Grahame Greene, author of *Brighton Rock*, *Our Man in Havana* and many other modern literary classics, named Bowen as a decisive influence on his early writing. Mark Twain and Arthur Conan Doyle were among her other admirers.

'"He Made a Woman—"' from Bowen's 1923 volume of stories *Seeing Life* focuses on the woods and myths of Wales, specifically Feryllwg, an ancient forest between the Wye and Severn rivers roughly equivalent to the Forest of Dean. While the Forest of Dean is today located in England, just across the border in Gloucestershire, in Bowen's story it is most definitely in Wales. Bowen's tale appears to draw on Lady Charlotte Guest's Victorian translation of *The Mabinogion*, a collection of the early narratives of Wales, written in Middle Welsh. In her extensive commentary on this important text, Guest suggests that Feryllwg "at one time formed a part of one of the five divisions of Wales" with the name "'Gwent Coch yn y Dena', or the *Red* Gwent in the Deans". Behind Bowen's mystical but ominous tale is the story of Blodeuwedd, "flower-face" in the Welsh (and also spelled Blodeuedd). Blodeuwedd was created by magicians to be the wife of Llew Llaw Gyffes, one of the great heroes of Welsh legend. Bowen blends traditional aspects of the Welsh myth with elements of science fiction and a touch of psychoanalysis; imagine *The Mabinogion* rewritten by H. G. Wells and then rewritten again by a disciple of Sigmund Freud. It is a curious but haunting tale that captures something of the sensuality of woodland.

"For many circumstances lead me to suspect that all these phenomena may depend upon certain forces, in virtue of which the particles of bodies, by causes not yet known, are either mutually impelled against one another and cohere into regular figures, or repel and recede from one another; which forces, being unknown, philosophers have as yet explored nature in vain."

—Sir Isaac Newton, preface to the *"Principia."*

dmund Charnock had reached that mental state when he could no longer endure even the worn comfort, the practical austerity of his favourite club; nerves and brain were too fine drawn, too weary of subtleties of thought and feeling; he was gorged with knowledge, disgusted with study, sick of his own personality.

Fame and wealth, luxury and amusement, seemed to him, not only paltry things—they even found some secret sense into agony.

Charnock was rather desperately aware that he must "get away"; but where?

The whole earth was so well known to him, and he could think of no spot remote enough, free enough from all association with threadbare human thoughts, inventions and emotions.

It was while he pondered this in the shabby, serene refuge of the favourite club that he met Blantyre, that wise, terrible, old scientist, whose intellect showed above that of the great ones of the world as the lofty pine shows above a clearing of weeds and bracken.

He was newly arrived from Roumania and was going to Wales; he had always been interested, in his cold, serene fashion, in Charnock, at one time a pupil of his, and he sat beside him now on the glossy, faded leather seat and let him talk, while he swung his eyeglasses at the end of the frayed black ribbon.

"I can't get hold of the reality of anything," said Charnock. "It's awful. Last night I dreamt I was handling a square heavy glass bottle—I *felt* it, saw the polish, the gleam, put my fingers up and down it—it was *real*—and all the time my hands were folded under my cheek. I dreamt I saw a bird, like a flying peacock, white in the air, grey when it descended—it was more real to me than anything I have seen since—I could draw it from memory—and all the while my eyes were closed. Now what *is* reality?"

"Perhaps there is no such thing," said Blantyre.

"But I must have something to hold to," answered Charnock.

"Why?—let yourself go."

"I dare not."

"Afraid? How strange." Blantyre smiled, increasing his myriad wrinkles. "I never could understand fear—"

"Not—fear of madness?"

"No."

Charnock sighed.

"I should like," he said, "to cease thinking, to cease knowing, to cease experiencing. My mind goes round and round like a squirrel in a cage—I am tired of the squirrel, irritated with the cage."

He stretched his long limbs and added—

"I must get hold of simplicity or become insane."

Blantyre glanced at him curiously.

"You are too young for what you have accomplished," he remarked.

"If only," said Charnock, "everything was not marked on a map—has that ever vexed you?—to think that there is no getting away from charts and maps?"

"They mean nothing," said Blantyre. "A few toys, that's all. Each generation has new toys, new jargon, new idols, new manners, that are all old toys, jargons and idols and manners rediscovered—what we call miracles are only unfamiliar happenings. We have forgotten so much. The Chaldeans would have found us provincial."

He paused; then added abruptly:

"Come with me to Wales. I think you would like my place."

Charnock accepted; he knew that Blantyre lived in scenes of complete isolation in a remote valley, among the hills haunted by many a mysterious legend, the setting of some of the oldest tales of Europe, and this disturbed him, for he was very sensitive to the influences of the past; yet for Blantyre's sake he went.

It was October; the strangest month in the year, Blantyre always said, culminating in the awful vigil of the last day which has some mystic meaning now lost.

As Charnock drove from the station through the wild ways and the thin wash of autumn sunshine he did feel a certain lift of the spirit, though faint and momentary. Blantyre told him that they were driving through the ancient Feryllwg, or Forest of Dean, which lies between the Wye and the Severn, and is full of oaks for ships and yews for archers; the part through which they turned was still unspoiled, he said, and he told Charnock tales of Llew Llaw Gyffes, one of the makers of gold-coloured shoes, and one of the crimson stained ones of the Island. And then the old man, as the quick pale dusk closed over them, said:

"I think I have not told you that I have my ward staying with me. She will not trouble you at all. She is a Welsh girl and has a Welsh name—Blodeuwedd—"

He looked at Charnock and added:

"The name means nothing to you if you do not know the bardic verses."

And Charnock replied that he had read these curious old fragments, but forgotten them, as he wished that he could forget his other cumbrous and vexing knowledge.

Blantyre went on describing the country, using the Welsh names and calling the forest Gwent Coch yn y Dena, in the country of Gwent, and he added that he had found no place in the world (and he had tried many) more soothing and reposeful than this odd corner of Wales; but Charnock could not agree, for already his restless imagination was peopling the autumn forest with old, far-off, grotesque figures, Arthur's fantastic knights, and Bran who went as hostage to Rome, and Lleufer Mawr, who built the first church in Britain, for he remembered these vaguely from readings long ago.

But Blantyre had made this ancient lore his recreation; his information was annoyingly exhaustive; he knew the crude old British tongue intimately, and he spoke much of a certain Gwydion ap Don, an older and more mighty magician than Merlin.

"Fairy tales," said Charnock peevishly.

"Well," smiled the old man, "isn't that what you want? Peace and simplicity?"

But to Charnock there was neither peace nor simplicity in all this, but the mere repetition of book wisdom, the jargon of the schools. Blantyre, thought the younger man with intense irritation, must have got into the way of it, and he had been a fool to think that he would find any real repose in the company of a pedant like Blantyre.

They reached the house when the moon was high amid light whirling clouds tossed by a frosty wind; it stood the far end of the forest on broken land surrounded by oak trees that swung and creaked in the gale.

"Remote enough," smiled Blantyre, "and crude enough for you to be able to forget your hothouse fancies."

Charnock felt the isolation and the roughness with a pang of relief; the icy air that blew sharply on him as he descended from the car, the moon so high and cold, the rude, square house of heavy stone set on the high piled rocks, the swift sound of an unseen stream, leaping from ledge to ledge until it gurgled into a forest pool—all this combined with one effect of wildness without fierceness, solitude without melancholy and strangeness without grotesqueness raised in Charnock a sense of quiet pleasure.

In the low, narrow doorway stood an old man holding a torch, the tawny glare of which was in rich contrast to the blue brilliance of the night; he stood aside to permit the two men to pass; the big car turned and sped back to civilisation.

Charnock gazed eagerly round a square room hung with coarse tapestry; there was a long oak table down the middle set with platters of wood, bottles and jugs of leather and knives of horn.

In an iron circlet held by iron chains to the beamed ceiling were stuck thick yellow candles all alight; on the huge open hearth burnt logs to a clear heart of fire, over which an elderly woman in a gown of black and white plaid, a heavy linen apron and 'kerchief, was standing and stirring the contents of an iron pot.

Blantyre spoke to his two servants in Welsh, and the woman left her cooking to show Charnock up the dark stairs to a large square room, with straw mattress and rugs, an ewer of water, a bowl and a stool, and a great window that looked on to the bright darkness of the night, the forest, the moon and the racing clouds.

As he gazed out on this noble prospect he was aware of what appeared to be a light female figure, that gave him an impression of a misty green and silver, moving rapidly over the rocks at the foot of the house; and he remembered with vexation that Blantyre had spoken of a woman—a ward.

When he went downstairs he saw her; she was seated at the table while the servant served out the supper, and Charnock saw her in the dim, wavering light of the circle of fat yellow candles.

She was of an almost nebulous fairness, her small face of a pale golden pallor, her gown of some archaic fashion, in hue changing tints of green.

Blantyre was reading aloud out of a book:

> "Hast thou heard what Llewlleaweg of Gwyddel sang,
> The noble chief wearing the golden tongues?
> 'The grave is better than a life of want.'
> Hast thou heard what Dremhidydd sang,
> An ancient watchman on the Castle walls?
> 'A refusal is better than a promise unperformed.'
> Hast thou heard what Beduini sang?
> A gifted Bishop of exalted rank?
> 'Consider thy word before it is given.'"

"This is Blodeuwedd," said Blantyre. "And you must promise me not to fall in love with her."

Charnock, the tall dark, cynical, thin man, smiled acridly; yet the old man spoke earnestly and with no offensiveness in his manner; he now wore a long, dark, tattered robe and a skull cap, and while they ate the primitive meal and drank the strong ale, he read aloud out of the big, soiled, worn book. Charnock watched the girl; she seldom moved and never spoke, her expression did not change, but she gave out life as light is given out from a clear, steady flame. To Charnock's weary mind she was symbolic of all the rest and serenity that he was in search of; he could not take his gaze from the hyacinth-white hues of her face, the knot of her pale gold hair, the soft, flowing, fluid lines of her body under her gown with the queer shifting shades of green.

After supper she left them; but Charnock continued to see her, even in his dreams.

Blantyre had a large laboratory built on to the ancient house, and there he spent most of his time, leaving the younger man full leisure to flavour the sharp, sweet, crude peace of the place, the cool, fresh presence of Blodeuwedd. Not that he often saw the girl, but her personality seemed to pervade the ancient house, the wild landscape, the changeful October weather.

Once or twice she spoke to him, but low and hesitating, like a child, and in the ancient language that he could not understand; and she never altered her gown, or her smile, or her bright still fragrance, her silent coming and going, her delicate, cheerful air of peace.

It was not what she was herself that so particularly pleased him as the manner in which she appeared to transform the entire world, as the sun will lighten the landscape, or the clear sky tint the ocean, or the perfume of flowers render every breeze a palpable thing.

She reminded him of some clouds he had seen once on a still winter night, so faint in the moonlight that they appeared but a wisp of lighter blue on the deep azure of the sky. Yet to them was all the magic of the night due. He spoke of her to Blantyre, and the old man reminded him of his dream of the square glass bottle and the grey, white peacock.

"Remember reality," he smiled. "You must not love this girl."

Charnock thought that he spoke foolishly, and wondered maliciously if the great brain was at last tottering into senility; he spent a great deal of time in his laboratory, and Charnock was content to be without his company, though he loathed the laboratory, this crude and ugly symbol of a dry search for bitter knowledge. At his warning about love Charnock always laughed; such talk was to the younger man a babble in an unknown tongue.

Love—any emotion any man could put such a man to—would never disturb his cold heart or soothe his restless mind… but what if the girl became necessary to him?

Supposing he felt he must always have her there, as some must always have a drug—a secret soporific?

His apprehension crept over him with an increasing dread; he could not, now, easily deny himself the girl's company, the pleasure of watching her, of being lulled in the elemental peace that enfolded her like a silver light.

She appeared to have no occupations, no cares, no arts, even no wits; she merely moved and smiled and made the day radiant.

To see her fold her gown about her long limbs, to knot up the yellow strings of her pallid hair, to watch her glimmer under the oak trees, spring from rock to rock beside the waterfall, lean over the rude board at meal times, bent above the ruddy fire in the evening—all these actions of hers were as draughts of Lethe to Charnock, his soul was lulled to a delicious drowsiness; he felt as if nothing had yet been and that he slept in a dim cavern while the world was created; he no longer dreaded nor feared civilisation, he ceased to be aware of it; he was no longer hag ridden by his learning, his experience; he began to forget all he had ever known. Once or twice he caught Blantyre's grin—wide, stretched, malevolent.

"Whatever are you doing in the laboratory?" he asked suddenly.

"Making experiments—experiments," smiled Blantyre. "My old experiments, too. Trying over again some of those of Gwydion ap Don——"

"Insane," thought Charnock with dislike.

"You should be here in the spring," continued Blantyre, "when the oaks are covered with bloom, the broom is in flower, and there bursts the first clusters of the meadowsweet."

As he spoke Blodeuwedd entered and stood by the rude window looking out on to the wide moonlight, which coloured her from head to foot with a pale greenish golden silver.

"Have you ever touched her?" asked Blantyre. "I wonder if she would bear the test of your dream, the square bottle?"

Charnock smiled; yet the old man's imbecility irritated him deeply.

"I must tell you about Gwydion," went on Blantyre; "he was a great magician; there is this rhyme about him; I have translated it thus—

> "Gwydion, the son of Don, of toil serene,
> He made a woman out of flowers
> Blossoms of broom, of oak, of meadowsweet."

Charnock interrupted with two sharp words, that leapt unbidden from some forgotten childhood.

"Jesu Christ!" he cried; he caught in a frantic grasp the green silver robe of Blodeuwedd. She vanished; there was a heavy coil of perfume in the air, and Charnock's thin hand grasped a spray of oak flower, a twig of broom, a cluster of meadowsweet.

THE FESTIVAL

H. P. Lovecraft

Howard Phillips Lovecraft (1890–1937) was born in Providence, Rhode Island, and lived most of his life in New England. When his father died of syphilis in 1898, he and his mother moved into her parental home. Lovecraft's interest in literature came from his maternal grandfather, who invented 'weird tales' for him. Lovecraft struggled with depression and other mental health issues throughout his life. His career as an author began as a result of writing critical letters to early pulp magazines, and he later started to submit stories of his own. At the time this story was published, he was living in a single room apartment in Brooklyn, New York, in poverty, and that same year was working on the outline for *The Call of Cthulhu*, a novelette which would later become one of his most influential works. Despite being regularly published in the magazine *Weird Tales* and elsewhere, he was not well known in his lifetime and struggled financially until his death at the age of 46 from cancer of the small intestine.

Today, whilst few would deny Lovecraft's huge importance as an influence on later horror, science fiction and fantasy writers, his legacy is tarnished by the racist, homophobic and misogynistic beliefs he held.

'Efficiunt Daemones, ut quae non sunt, sic tamen quasi sint, conspicienda hominibus exhibeant.'

—*Lactantius.*

was far from home, and the spell of the eastern sea was upon me. In the twilight I heard it pounding on the rocks, and I knew it lay just over the hill where the twisting willows writhed against the clearing sky and the first stars of evening. And because my fathers had called me to the old town beyond, I pushed on through the shallow, new-fallen snow along the road that soared lonely up to where Aldebaran twinkled among the trees; on toward the very ancient town I had never seen but often dreamed of.

It was the Yuletide, that men call Christmas though they know in their hearts it is older than Bethlehem and Babylon, older than Memphis and mankind. It was the Yuletide, and I had come at last to the ancient sea town where my people had dwelt and kept festival in the elder time when festival was forbidden; where also they had commanded their sons to keep festival once every century, that the memory of primal secrets might not be forgotten. Mine were an old people, and were old even when this land was settled three hundred years before. And they were strange, because they had come as dark furtive folk from opiate southern gardens of orchids, and spoken another tongue before they learnt the tongue of the blue-eyed fishers. And now they were scattered, and shared only the rituals of mysteries that none living could understand. I was the only one who came back that night to the old fishing town as legend bade, for only the poor and the lonely remember.

Then beyond the hill's crest I saw Kingsport outspread frostily in the gloaming; snowy Kingsport with its ancient vanes and steeples, ridgepoles and chimney-pots, wharves and small bridges, willow-trees and graveyards; endless labyrinths of steep, narrow, crooked streets, and dizzy church-crowned central peak that time durst not touch; ceaseless mazes of colonial houses piled and scattered at all angles and levels like a child's disordered blocks; antiquity hovering on grey wings over winter-whitened gables and gambrel roofs; fanlights and small-paned windows one by one gleaming out in the cold dusk to join Orion and the archaic stars. And against the rotting wharves the sea pounded; the secretive, immemorial sea out of which the people had come in the elder time.

Beside the road at its crest a still higher summit rose, bleak and windswept, and I saw that it was a burying-ground where black gravestones stuck ghoulishly through the snow like the decayed fingernails of a gigantic corpse. The printless road was very lonely, and sometimes I thought I heard a distant horrible creaking as of a gibbet in the wind. They had hanged four kinsmen of mine for witchcraft in 1692, but I did not know just where.

As the road wound down the seaward slope I listened for the merry sounds of a village at evening, but did not hear them. Then I thought of the season, and felt that these old Puritan folk might well have Christmas customs strange to me, and full of silent hearth-side prayer. So after that I did not listen for merriment or look for wayfarers, but kept on down past the hushed lighted farmhouses and shadowy stone walls to where the signs of ancient shops and sea-taverns creaked in the salt breeze, and the grotesque knockers of pillared doorways glistened along deserted, unpaved lanes in the light of little, curtained windows.

I had seen maps of the town, and knew where to find the home of my people. It was told that I should be known and welcomed, for village legend lives long; so I hastened through Back Street to Circle Court, and across the fresh snow on the one full flagstone pavement in the town, to where Green Lane leads off behind the Market House. The old maps still held good, and I had no trouble; though at Arkham they must have lied when they said the trolleys ran to this place, since I saw not a wire overhead. Snow would have hid the rails in any case. I was glad I had chosen to walk, for the white village had seemed very beautiful from the hill; and now I was eager to knock at the door of my people, the seventh house on the left in Green Lane, with an ancient peaked roof and jutting second storey, all built before 1650.

There were lights inside the house when I came upon it, and I saw from the diamond window-panes that it must have been kept very close to its antique state. The upper part overhung the narrow grass-grown street and nearly met the overhanging part of the house opposite, so that I was almost in a tunnel, with the low stone doorstep wholly free from snow. There was no sidewalk, but many houses had high doors reached by double flights of steps with iron railings. It was an odd scene, and because I was strange to New England I had never known its like before. Though it pleased me, I would have relished it better if there had been footprints in the snow, and people in the streets, and a few windows without drawn curtains.

When I sounded the archaic iron knocker I was half afraid. Some fear had been gathering in me, perhaps because of the strangeness of my heritage, and the bleakness of the evening, and the queerness of the silence in that aged town of curious customs. And when my knock was answered I was fully afraid, because I had not heard any footsteps before the door creaked open. But I was not afraid long, for the gowned, slippered old man in the doorway had a bland face that reassured me; and though he made signs that he was dumb, he wrote a quaint and ancient welcome with the stylus and wax tablet he carried.

He beckoned me into a low, candle-lit room with massive exposed rafters and dark, stiff, sparse furniture of the seventeenth century. The past was vivid there, for not an attribute was missing. There was a cavernous fireplace and a spinning-wheel at which a bent old woman in loose wrapper and deep poke-bonnet sat back toward me, silently spinning despite the festive season. An indefinite dampness seemed upon the place, and I marvelled that no fire should be blazing. The high-backed settle faced the row of curtained windows at the left, and seemed to be occupied, though I was not sure. I did not like everything about what I saw, and felt again the fear I had had. This fear grew stronger from what had before lessened it, for the more I looked at the old man's bland face the more its very blandness terrified me. The eyes never moved, and the skin was too like wax. Finally I was sure it was not a face at all, but a fiendishly cunning mask. But the flabby hands, curiously gloved, wrote genially on the tablet and told me I must wait a while before I could be led to the place of the festival.

Pointing to a chair, table, and pile of books, the old man now left the room; and when I sat down to read I saw that the books were hoary and mouldy, and that they included old Morryster's wild 'Marvells of Science', the terrible 'Saducismus Triumphatus' of Joseph Glanvill, published in 1681, the shocking 'Daemonolatreia' of Remigius, printed in 1595 at Lyons, and worst of all, the unmentionable 'Necronomicon' of the mad Arab Abdul Alhazred, in Olaus Wormius' forbidden Latin translation; a book which I had never seen, but of which I had heard monstrous things whispered. No one spoke to me, but I could hear the creaking of signs in the wind outside, and the whir of the wheel as the bonneted old woman continued her silent spinning, spinning. I thought the room and the books and the people very morbid and disquieting, but because an old tradition of my fathers had summoned me to strange feastings, I resolved to expect queer things. So I tried to read, and soon became tremblingly absorbed by something I found in that accursed 'Necronomicon'; a thought and a legend too hideous for sanity or consciousness. But I disliked it when I fancied I heard the closing of one of the windows that the settle faced, as if it had been stealthily opened. It had seemed to follow a whirring that was not of the old woman's spinning-wheel. This was not much, though, for the old woman was spinning very hard, and the aged clock had been striking. After that I lost the feeling that there were persons on the settle, and was reading intently and shudderingly when the old man came back booted and dressed in a loose antique costume, and sat down on that very bench, so that I could not see him. It was certainly nervous waiting, and the blasphemous book in my hands made it doubly so. When eleven struck, however, the old man stood up, glided to a massive carved chest in a corner, and got two hooded cloaks; one of which he donned, and the other of which he draped round the old woman, who was ceasing her monotonous spinning. Then they both started for the outer door; the woman lamely creeping, and the old man, after picking up the very book I had been reading, beckoning me as he drew his hood over that unmoving face or mask.

We went out into the moonless and tortuous network of that incredibly ancient town; went out as the lights in the curtained windows disappeared one by one, and the Dog Star leered at the throng of cowled, cloaked figures that poured silently from every doorway and formed monstrous processions up this street and that, past the creaking signs and antediluvian gables, the thatched roofs and diamond-paned windows; threading precipitous lanes where decaying houses overlapped and crumbled together, gliding across open courts and churchyards where the bobbing lanthorns made eldritch drunken constellations.

Amid these hushed throngs I followed my voiceless guides; jostled by elbows that seemed preternaturally soft, and pressed by chests and stomachs that seemed abnormally pulpy; but seeing never a face and hearing never a word. Up, up, up the eery columns slithered, and I saw that all the travellers were converging as they flowed near a sort of focus of crazy alleys at the top of a high hill in the centre of the town, where perched a great white church. I had seen it from the road's crest when I looked at Kingsport in the new dusk, and it had made me shiver because Aldebaran had seemed to balance itself a moment on the ghostly spire.

There was an open space around the church; partly a churchyard with spectral shafts, and partly a half-paved square swept nearly bare of snow by the wind, and lined with unwholesomely archaic houses having peaked roofs and overhanging gables. Death-fires danced over the tombs, revealing gruesome vistas, though queerly failing to cast any shadows. Past the churchyard, where there were no houses, I could see over the hill's summit and watch the glimmer of stars on the harbour, though the town was invisible in the dark. Only once in a while a lanthorn bobbed horribly through serpentine alleys on its way to overtake the throng that was now slipping speechlessly into the church. I waited till the crowd had oozed into the black doorway, and till all the stragglers had followed. The old man was pulling at my sleeve, but I was determined to be the last. Then finally I went, the sinister man and the old spinning woman before me. Crossing the threshold into that swarming temple of unknown darkness, I turned once to look at the outside world as the church-yard phosphorescence cast a sickly glow on the hilltop pavement. And as I did so I shuddered. For though the wind had not left much snow, a few patches did remain on the path near the door; and in that fleeting backward look it seemed to my troubled eyes that they bore no mark of passing feet, not even mine.

The church was scarce lighted by all the lanthorns that had entered it, for most of the throng had already vanished. They had streamed up the aisle between the high white pews to the trap-door of the vaults which yawned loathsomely open just before the pulpit, and were now squirming noiselessly in. I followed dumbly down the footworn steps and into the dank, suffocating crypt. The tail of that sinuous line of night-marchers seemed very horrible, and as I saw them wriggling into a venerable tomb they seemed more horrible still. Then I noticed that the tomb's floor had an aperture down which the throng was sliding, and in a moment we were all descending an ominous staircase of rough-hewn stone; a narrow spiral staircase damp and peculiarly odorous, that wound endlessly down into the bowels of the hill past monotonous walls of dripping stone blocks and crumbling mortar. It was a silent, shocking descent, and I observed after a horrible interval that the walls and steps were changing in nature, as if chiselled out of the solid rock. What mainly troubled me was that the myriad footfalls made no sound and set up no echoes. After more aeons of descent I saw some side passages or burrows leading from unknown recesses of blackness to this shaft of nighted mystery. Soon they became excessively numerous, like impious catacombs of nameless menace; and their pungent odour of decay grew quite unbearable. I knew we must have passed down through the mountain and beneath the earth of Kingsport itself, and I shivered that a town should be so aged and maggoty with subterraneous evil.

Then I saw the lurid shimmering of pale light, and heard the insidious lapping of sunless waters. Again I shivered, for I did not like the things that the night had brought, and wished bitterly that no forefather had summoned me to this primal rite. As the steps and the passage grew broader, I heard another sound, the thin, whining mockery of a feeble flute; and suddenly there spread out before me the boundless vista of an inner world—a vast fungous shore litten by a belching column of sick greenish flame and washed by a wide oily river that flowed from abysses frightful and unsuspected to join the blackest gulfs of immemorial ocean.

Fainting and gasping, I looked at that unhallowed Erebus of titan toadstools, leprous fire, and slimy water, and saw the cloaked throngs forming a semicircle around the blazing pillar. It was the Yule-rite, older than man and fated to survive him; the primal rite of the solstice and of spring's promise beyond the snows; the rite of fire and evergreen, light and music. And in that Stygian grotto I saw them do the rite, and adore the sick pillar of flame, and throw into the water handfuls gouged out of the viscous vegetation which glittered green in the chlorotic glare. I saw this, and I saw something amorphously squatted far away from the light, piping noisomely on a flute; and as the thing piped I thought I heard noxious muffled flutterings in the foetid darkness where I could not see. But what frightened me most was that flaming column; spouting volcanically from depths profound and inconceivable, casting no shadows as healthy flame should, and coating the nitrous stone above with a nasty, venomous verdigris. For in all that seething combustion no warmth lay, but only the clamminess of death and corruption.

The man who had brought me now squirmed to a point directly beside the hideous flame, and made stiff ceremonial motions to the semicircle he faced. At certain stages of the ritual they did grovelling obeisance, especially when he held above his head that abhorrent 'Necronomicon' he had taken with him; and I shared all the obeisances because I had been summoned to this festival by the writings of my forefathers. Then the old man made a signal to the half-seen flute-player in the darkness, which player thereupon changed its feeble drone to a scarce louder drone in another key; precipitating as it did so a horror unthinkable and unexpected. At this horror I sank nearly to the lichened earth, transfixed with a dread not of this nor any world, but only of the mad spaces between the stars.

Out of the unimaginable blackness beyond the gangrenous glare of that cold flame, out of the tartarean leagues through which that oily river rolled uncanny, unheard, and unsuspected, there flopped rhythmically a horde of tame, trained, hybrid winged things that no sound eye could ever wholly grasp, or sound brain ever wholly remember. They were not altogether crows, nor moles, nor buzzards, nor ants, nor vampire bats, nor decomposed human beings;

but something I cannot and must not recall. They flopped limply along, half with their webbed feet and half with their membraneous wings; and as they reached the throng of celebrants the cowled figures seized and mounted them, and rode off one by one along the reaches of that unlighted river, into pits and galleries of panic where poison springs feed frightful and undiscoverable cataracts.

The old spinning woman had gone with the throng, and the old man remained only because I had refused when he motioned me to seize an animal and ride like the rest. I saw when I staggered to my feet that the amorphous flute-player had rolled out of sight, but that two of the beasts were patiently standing by. As I hung back, the old man produced his stylus and tablet and wrote that he was the true deputy of my fathers who had founded the Yule worship in this ancient place; that it had been decreed I should come back, and that the most secret mysteries were yet to be performed. He wrote this in a very ancient hand, and when I still hesitated he pulled from his loose robe a seal ring and a watch, both with my family arms, to prove that he was what he said. But it was a hideous proof, because I knew from old papers that that watch had been buried with my great-great-great-great-grandfather in 1698.

Presently the old man drew back his hood and pointed to the family resemblance in his face, but I only shuddered, because I was sure that the face was merely a devilish waxen mask. The flopping animals were now scratching restlessly at the lichens, and I saw that the old man was nearly as restless himself. When one of the things began to waddle and edge away, he turned quickly to stop it; so that the suddenness of his motion dislodged the waxen mask from what should have been his head. And then, because that nightmare's position barred me from the stone staircase down which we had come, I flung myself into the oily underground river that bubbled somewhere to the caves of the sea; flung myself into that putrescent juice of earth's inner horrors before the madness of my screams could bring down upon me all the charnel legions these pest-gulfs might conceal.

At the hospital they told me I had been found half-frozen in Kingsport Harbour at dawn, clinging to the drifting spar that accident sent to save me. They told me I had taken the wrong fork of the hill road the night before, and fallen over the cliffs at Orange Point; a thing they deduced from prints found in the snow. There was nothing I could say, because everything was wrong. Everything was wrong, with the broad window shewing a sea of roofs in which only about one in five was ancient, and the sound of trolleys and motors in the streets below. They insisted that this was Kingsport, and I could not deny it. When I went delirious at hearing that the hospital stood near the old churchyard on Central Hill, they sent me to St. Mary's Hospital in Arkham, where I could have better care. I liked it there, for the doctors were broad-minded, and even lent me their influence in obtaining the carefully sheltered copy of Alhazred's objectionable 'Necronomicon' from the library of Miskatonic University. They said something about a 'psychosis', and agreed I had better get any harassing obsessions off my mind.

So I read again that hideous chapter, and shuddered doubly because it was indeed not new to me. I had seen it before, let footprints tell what they might; and where it was I had seen it were best forgotten. There was no one—in waking hours—who could remind me of it; but my dreams are filled with terror, because of phrases I dare not quote. I dare quote only one paragraph, put into such English as I can make from the awkward Low Latin.

III

'The nethermost caverns,' wrote the mad Arab, 'are not for the fathoming of eyes that see; for their marvels are strange and terrific. Cursed the ground where dead thoughts live new and oddly bodied, and evil the mind that is held by no head. Wisely did Ibn Schacabao say, that happy is the tomb where no wizard hath lain, and happy the town at night whose wizards are all ashes. For it is of old rumour that the soul of the devil-bought hastes not from his charnel clay, but fats and instructs *the very worm that gnaws;* till out of corruption horrid life springs, and the dull scavengers of earth wax crafty to vex it and swell monstrous to plague it. Great holes secretly are digged where earth's pores ought to suffice, and things have learnt to walk that ought to crawl.'

THE THREE MARKED PENNIES

Mary E. Counselman

Counselman was an American poet and short-story writer who became known as "The Queen of *Weird Tales*" because of the popularity of her thirty stories in that magazine. She contributed to many magazines, including *Collier's Weekly*, *Saturday Evening Post*, *Jungle Stories* and *Thrilling Mystery*, but it was her appearances in *Weird Tales* that made her work memorable. Her first story there was "The House of Shadows" (1933), and several stories, including "The Shot-Tower Ghost" (1949) and "The Green Window" (1949), were inspired by her own direct experiences. Her best-known story, "The Three Marked Pennies", which is reprinted here, was highlighted as one of the most popular ever published in *Weird Tales*. Several of her strange stories were collected in *Half in Shadow* (1964; reprinted with several different stories in 1978), whilst *African Yesterdays* (1975) brings together many of her stories based on native African folklore.

veryone agreed, after it was over, that the whole thing was the conception of a twisted brain, a game of chess played by a madman—in which the pieces, instead of carved bits of ivory or ebony, were human beings.

It was odd that no one doubted the authenticity of the "contest." The public seems never for a moment to have considered it the prank of a practical joker, or even a publicity stunt. Jeff Haverty, editor of the *News*, advanced a theory that the affair was meant to be a clever, if rather elaborate, psychological experiment—which would end in the revealing of the originator's identity and a big laugh for everyone.

Perhaps it was the glamorous manner of announcement that gave the thing such widespread interest. Branton, the southern town of about thirty thousand people in which the affair occurred, awoke one April morning to find all its trees, telephone poles, house-sides, and storefronts plastered with a strange sign. There were scores of them, written on yellow copy-paper on an ordinary typewriter. The sign read:

> "During this day of April 15, three pennies will find their way into the pockets of this city. On each penny there will be a well-defined mark. One is a square; one is a circle; and one is a cross. These three pennies will change hands often, as do all coins, and on the seventh day after this announcement (April 21) the possessor of each marked penny will receive a gift.
>
> "To the first: $100,000 in cash.
>
> "To the second: A trip around the world.

"To the third: Death.

"The answer to this riddle lies in the marks on the three coins: circle, square, and cross. Which of these symbolizes wealth? Which, travel? Which, death? The answer is not an obvious one.

"To him who finds it and obtains the first penny, $100,000 will be sent without delay. To him who has the second penny, a first-class ticket for the earliest world-touring steamer to sail will be presented. But to the possessor of the third marked coin will be given—death. If you are afraid your penny is the third, give it away—but it may be the first or the second!

"Show your marked penny to the editor of the 'News' on April 21, giving your name and address. He will know nothing of this contest until he reads one of these signs. He is requested to publish the names of the three possessors of the coins April 21, with the mark on the penny each holds.

"It will do no good to mark a coin of your own, as the dates of the true coins will be sent to Editor Haverty."

By noon everyone had read the notice, and the city was buzzing with excitement. Clerks began to examine the contents of cash register drawers. Hands rummaged in pockets and purses. Stores and banks were flooded with customers wanting silver changed to coppers.

Jeff Haverty was the target for a barrage of queries, and his evening edition came with a lengthy editorial embodying all he knew about the mystery, which was exactly nothing. A note had come that morning with the rest of his mail—a note unsigned, and typewritten on the same yellow paper in a plain stamped envelope with the postmark of that city. It said merely: *"Circle—1920. Square—1909. Cross—1928. Please do not reveal these dates until after April 21."*

Haverty complied with the request, and played up the story for all it was worth.

The first penny was found in the street by a small boy, who promptly took it to his father. His father, in turn, palmed it off hurriedly on his barber, who gave it in change to a patron before he noted the deep cross cut in the coin's surface.

The patron took it to his wife, who immediately paid it to the grocer. "It's too long a chance, honey!" she silenced her mate's protests. "I don't like the idea of that death-threat in the notice... and this certainly must be the third penny. What else could that little cross stand for? Crosses over graves—don't you see the significance?"

And when that explanation was wafted abroad, the cross-marked penny began to change hands with increasing rapidity.

The other two pennies bobbed up before dusk—one marked with a small perfect square, the other with a neat circle.

The square-marked penny was discovered in a slot-machine by the proprietor of the Busy Bee Café. There was no way it could have got there, he reported, mystified and a little frightened. Only four people, all of them old patrons, had been in the café that day. And not one of them had been near the slot-machine—located at the back of the place as it was, and filled with stale chewing-gum which, at a glance, was worth nobody's penny. Furthermore, the proprietor had examined the thing for a chance coin the night before and had left it empty when he locked up; yet there was the square-marked penny nestling alone in the slot-machine at closing time April fifteenth.

He had stared at the coin a long time before passing it in change to an elderly spinster.

"It ain't worth it," he muttered to himself. "I got a restaurant that's makin' me a thin livin', and I ain't in no hurry to get myself bumped off, on the long chance I might get that hundred thousand or that trip instead. No-sirree!"

The spinster took one look at the marked penny, gave a short mouselike squeak, and flung it into the gutter as though it were a tarantula.

"My land!" she quavered. "I don't want that thing in my pocket-book!"

But she dreamed that night of foreign ports, of dockhands jabbering in a brittle tongue, of barracuda fins cutting the surface of deep blue water, and the ruins of ancient cities.

A workman picked up the penny next morning and clung to it all day, dreaming of Harlem, before he succumbed at last to gnawing fear. And the square-marked penny changed hands once more.

The circle-marked penny was first noted in a stack of coins by a teller of the Farmer's Trust.

"We get marked coins every now and then," he said. "I didn't notice this one especially—it may have been here for days."

He pocketed it gleefully, but discovered with a twinge of dismay next morning that he had passed it out to someone without noticing it.

"I wanted to keep it!" he sighed. "For better or for worse!"

He glowered at the stacks of someone else's money before him, and wondered furtively how many tellers really escaped with stolen goods.

A fruit-seller had received the penny. He eyed it dubiously. "Mebbe you bring-a me those mon, heh?" He showed it to his fat, greasy wife, who made the sign of horns against the "evil eye."

"T'row away!" she commanded shrilly. "She iss bad lock!"

Her spouse shrugged and sailed the circle-marked coin across the street. A ragged child pounced on it and scuttered away to buy a twist of licorice. And the circle-marked penny changed hands once more—clutched at by avaricious fingers, stared at by eyes grown sick of familiar scenes, relinquished again by the power of fear.

Those who came into brief possession of the three coins were fretted by the drag and shove of conflicting advice.

"Keep it!" some urged. "Think! It may mean a trip around the world! Paris! China! London! Oh, why couldn't I have got the thing?"

"Give it away!" others admonished. "Maybe it's the third penny—you can't tell. Maybe the symbols don't mean what they seem to, and the square one is the death-penny! I'd throw it away, if I were you."

"No! No!" still others cried. "Hang on to it! It may bring you $100,000. *A hundred thousand dollars!* In these times! Why, fellow, you'd be the same as a millionaire!"

The meaning of the three symbols was on everyone's tongue, and no one agreed with his neighbour's solution to the riddle.

"It's as plain as the nose on my face," one man would declare. "The circle represents the globe—the travel-penny, see?"

"No, no. The cross means that. 'Cross' the seas, don't you get it? Sort of a pun effect. The circle means money—shape of a coin, understand?"

"And the square one—?"

"A grave. A square hole for a coffin, see? Death. It's quite simple. I wish I could get hold of that circle one!"

"You're crazy! The cross one is for death—everybody says so. And believe me, everybody's getting rid of it as soon as they get it! It may be a joke of some kind... no danger at all... but I wouldn't like to be the holder of that cross-marked penny when April twenty-first rolls around!"

"I'd keep it and wait till the other two had got what was due them. Then, if mine turned out to be the wrong one, I'd throw it away!" one man said importantly.

"But he won't pay up till all three pennies are accounted for, I shouldn't think," another answered him. "And maybe the offer doesn't hold good after April twenty-first—and you'd be losing the hundred thousand dollars or a world tour just because you're scared to find out!"

"That's a big stake, man," another murmured. "But frankly, I wouldn't like to take the chance. He might give me his third gift!"

"He" was how everyone designated the unknown originator of the contest; though, of course, there was no more clue to his sex than to his identity.

"He must be rich," some said, "to offer such expensive prizes."

"And crazy!" others exploded, "threatening to kill the third one. He'll never get away with it!"

"But clever," still others admitted, "to think up the whole business. He knows human nature, whoever he is. I'm inclined to agree with Haverty—it's all a sort of psychological experiment. He's trying to see whether desire for travel or greed for money is stronger than fear of death."

"Does he mean to pay up, do you think?"

"That remains to be seen!"

On the sixth day, Branton had reached a pitch of excitement amounting almost to hysteria. No one could work for wondering about the outcome of the bizarre test on the morrow.

It was known that a grocer's delivery boy held the square-marked coin, for he had been boasting of his indifference as to whether or not the square did represent a yawning grave. He exhibited the penny freely, making jokes about what he intended to do with his hundred thousand dollars—but on the morning of the last day he lost his nerve. Seeing a blind beggar woman huddled in her favourite corner between two shops, he passed close to her and surreptitiously dropped the cent piece into her box of pencils.

"I had it!" he wailed to a friend after he had reached his grocery. "I had it right here in my pocket last night, and now it's gone! See, I've got a hole in the dam' thing—the penny must have dropped out!"

It was also known who held the circle-marked penny. A young soda-clerk, with the sort of ready smile that customers like to see across a marble counter, had discovered the coin and fished it from the cash drawer, exulting over his good fortune.

"Bud Skinner's got the circle penny," people told one another, wavering between anxiety and gladness. "I hope the kid *does* get that world tour—it'd tickle him so! He seems to get such a kick out of life; it's a sin he has to be stuck in this slow burg!"

Finally it was found who held the cross-marked cent piece. "Carlton... poor devil!" people murmured in subdued tones. "Death would be a godsend to him. Wonder he hasn't shot himself before this. Guess he just hasn't the nerve."

The man with the cross-marked penny smiled bitterly. "I hope this blasted little symbol means what they all think it means!" he confided to a friend.

At last the eagerly awaited day came. A crowd formed in the street outside the newspaper office to see the three possessors of the three marked coins show Haverty their pennies and give him their names to publish. For their benefit the editor met the trio on the sidewalk outside the building, so that all might see them.

The evening edition ran the three people's photographs, with the name, address, and the mark on each one's penny under each picture. Branton read... and held its breath.

On the morning of April twenty-second, the old blind beggar woman sat in her accustomed place, musing on the excitement of the previous day, when several people had led her—she knew by the odour of fish from the market across the street—to the newspaper office. There someone had asked her name and many other puzzling things which had bewildered her until she had almost burst into tears.

"Let me alone!" she had whimpered. "I ask only enough food to keep from starving, and a place to sleep. Why are you pushing me around like this and yelling at me? Let me go back to my corner! I don't like all this confusion and strangeness that I can't see—it frightens me!"

Then they had told her something about a marked penny they had found in her alms-box, and other things about a large sum of money and some impending danger that threatened her. She was glad when they led her back to her cranny between the shops.

Now as she sat in her accustomed spot, nodding comfortably and humming a little under her breath, a paper fluttered down into her lap. She felt the stiff oblong, knew it was an envelope, and called a bystander to her side.

"Open this for me, will you?" she requested. "Is it a letter? Read it to me."

The bystander tore open the envelope and frowned. "It's a note," he told her. "Typewritten, and it's not signed. It just says—what the devil?—just says: '*The four corners of the earth are exactly the same.*' And... hey! look at this!... oh, I'm sorry; I forgot you're... it's a steamship ticket for a world tour! Look, didn't you have one of the marked pennies?"

The blind woman nodded drowsily. "Yes, the one with the square, they said." She sighed faintly. "I had hoped I would get the money, or... the other, so I would never have to beg again."

"Well, here's your ticket." The bystander held it out to her uncertainly. "Don't you want it?" as the beggar made no move to take it.

"No," snapped the blind woman. "What good would it be to me?" She seized the ticket in sudden rage, and tore it into bits.

At nearly the same hour, Kenneth Carlton was receiving a fat manila envelope from the postman. He frowned as he squinted at the local postmark over the stamp. His friend Evans stood beside him, paler than Carlton.

"Open it, open it!" he urged. "Read it—no, don't open it, Ken. I'm scared! After all... it's a terrible way to go. Not knowing where the blow's coming from, and—"

Carlton emitted a macabre chuckle, ripping open the heavy envelope. "It's the best break I've had in years, Jim. I'm glad! Glad, Jim, do you hear? It will be quick, I hope... and painless. What's this, I wonder. A treatise on how to blow off the top of your head?" He shook the contents of the letter onto a table, and then, after a moment, he began to laugh... mirthlessly... hideously.

His friend stared at the little heap of crisp bills, all of a larger denomination than he had ever seen before. "The money! You get the hundred thousand, Ken! I can't believe..." He broke off to snatch up a slip of yellow paper among the bills. "*Wealth is the greatest cross a man can bear,*" he read aloud the typewritten words.

"It doesn't make sense... wealth? Then... the cross-mark stood for wealth? I don't understand."

Carlton's laughter cracked. "He has depth, that bird—whoever he is! Nice irony there, Jim—wealth being a burden instead of the blessing most people consider it. I suppose he's right, at that. But I wonder if he knows the really ironic part of this act of his little play? A hundred thousand dollars to a man with—cancer. Well, Jim, I have a month or less to spend it in... one more damnable month to suffer through before it's all over!"

His terrible laughter rose again, until his friend had to clap hands to ears, shutting out the sound.

But the strangest part of the whole affair was Bud Skinner's death. Just after the rush hour at noon, he had found a small package, addressed to him, on a back counter in the drug store. Eagerly he tore off the brown paper wrappings, a dozen or so friends crowding around him.

A curiously wrought silver box was what he found. He pressed the catch with trembling fingers and snapped back the lid. An instant later his face took on a queer expression—and he slid noiselessly to the tile floor of the drug store.

The ensuing police investigation unearthed nothing at all, except that young Skinner had been poisoned with *crotalin*—snake venom—administered through a pin-prick on his thumb when he pressed the trick catch on the little silver box. This, and the typewritten note in the otherwise empty box: "*Life ends where it began—nowhere,*" were all they found as an explanation of the clerk's death. Nor was anything else ever brought to light about the mysterious contest of the three marked pennies—which are probably still in circulation somewhere in the United States.

THE VISITING STAR

Robert Aickman

Robert Fordyce Aickman (1914–1981) is best known as both a writer of what he called 'strange stories' and as a campaigner for the preservation of England's canal system. He was the grandson of Richard Marsh, whose horror novel *The Beetle* outsold Bram Stoker's *Dracula* in 1897, the year they were both published. The Oxford Dictionary of National Biography describes the rather odd basis of Aickman's early life:

'Richard Marsh met William Arthur Aickman in the gentlemen's lavatory of a grand hotel in Edwardian Eastbourne, and was soon to encourage his marriage to his younger daughter, thirty years William Arthur Aickman's junior. The marriage, and Aickman's childhood, was predictably unhappy.'

In 1951, whilst working as a literary agent in Bloomsbury, Aickman penned a collection of ghost tales called *We are for the Dark* (together with the novelist Elizabeth Jane Howard). He went on to become a prolific writer of the genre, publishing eleven collections of his own stories. They are characterized by an extremely unsettling nightmarish weirdness. This is one of very few Christmas-themed tales he produced, and it draws on his strong interest in and enthusiasm for the theatre.

he first time that Colvin, who had never been a frequent theatre-goer, ever heard of the great actress Arabella Rokeby was when he was walking past the Hippodrome one night and Malnik, the Manager of the Tabard Players, invited him into his office.

Had Colvin not been awarded a grant, remarkably insufficient for present prices, upon which to compose, collate, and generally scratch together a book upon the once thriving British industries of lead and plumbago mining, he would probably never have set eyes upon this bleak town. Tea was over (today it had been pilchard salad and chips); and Colvin had set out from the Emancipation Hotel, where he boarded, upon his regular evening walk. In fifteen or twenty minutes he would be beyond the gas-lights, the granite setts, the nimbus of the pits. (Lead and plumbago mining had long been replaced by coal as the town's main industry.) There had been no one else for tea and Mrs Royd had made it clear that the trouble he was causing had not passed unnoticed.

Outside it was blowing as well as raining, so that Palmerston Street was almost deserted. The Hippodrome (called, when built, the Grand Opera House) stood at the corner of Palmerston Street and Aberdeen Place. Vast, ornate, the product of an unfulfilled aspiration that the town would increase in size and devotion to the Muses, it had been for years unused and forgotten. About it like rags, when Colvin first beheld it, had hung scraps of posters: 'Harem Nights. Gay! Bright! ! Alluring ! ! !' But a few weeks ago the Hippodrome had reopened to admit the Tabard Players ('In Association with the Arts Council'); and, it was hoped, their audiences. The Tabard Players offered soberer joys: a new and respectable play each week, usually a light comedy or West End crook drama; but, on one occasion, *Everyman*. Malnik, their Manager, a youngish bald man, was an authority on the British Drama of the Nineteenth Century, upon which he had written an immense book, bursting with carefully verified detail. Colvin had met him one night in the Saloon Bar of the Emancipation Hotel; and, though neither knew anything of the other's subject, they had exchanged cultural life-belts in the ocean of apathy and incomprehensible interests which surrounded them. Malnik was lodging with the sad-faced Rector, who let rooms.

Tonight, having seen the curtain up on Act I, Malnik had come outside for a breath of the wind. There was something he wanted to impart; and, as he regarded the drizzling and indifferent town, Colvin obligingly came into sight. In a moment, he was inside Malnik's roomy but crumbling office.

'Look,' said Malnik.

He shuffled a heap of papers on his desk and handed Colvin a photograph. It was yellow, and torn at the edges. The subject was a wild-eyed young man with much dark curly hair and a blobby face. He was wearing a high stiff collar, and a bow like Chopin's.

'John Nethers,' said Malnik. Then, when no light of rapture flashed from Colvin's face, he said 'Author of *Cornelia*.'

'Sorry,' said Colvin, shaking his head.

'John Nethers was the son of a chemist in this town. Some books say a miner, but that's wrong. A chemist. He killed himself at twenty-two. But before that I've traced that he'd written at least six plays. *Cornelia*, which is the best of them, is one of the great plays of the nineteenth century.'

'Why did he kill himself?'

'It's in his eyes. You can see it. *Cornelia* was produced in London with Arabella Rokeby. But never here. Never in the author's own town. I've been into the whole thing closely. Now we're going to do *Cornelia* for Christmas.'

'Won't you lose money?' asked Colvin.

'We're losing money all the time, old man. Of course we are. We may as well do something we shall be remembered by.'

Colvin nodded. He was beginning to see that Malnik's life was a single-minded struggle for the British Drama of the Nineteenth Century and all that went with it.

'Besides I'm going to do *As You Like It* also. As a fill-up.' Malnik stooped and spoke close to Colvin's ear as he sat in a bursting leather armchair, the size of a Judge's seat. 'You see, Arabella Rokeby's *coming.*'

'But how long is it since—'

'Better not be too specific about that. They say it doesn't matter with Arabella Rokeby. She can get away with it. Probably in fact she can't. Not altogether. But all the same, think of it. Arabella Rokeby in *Cornelia*. In my theatre.'

Colvin thought of it.

'Have you ever seen her?'

'No, I haven't. Of course she doesn't play regularly nowadays. Only special engagements. But in this business one has to take a chance sometimes. And golly what a chance!'

'And she's willing to come? I mean at Christmas,' Colvin added, not wishing to seem rude.

Malnik did seem slightly unsure. 'I have a contract,' he said. Then he added: 'She'll love it when she gets here. After all:

Cornelia! And she must know that the nineteenth-century theatre is my subject.' He had seemed to be reassuring himself, but now he was glowing.

'But *As You Like It?*' said Colvin, who had played Touchstone at his preparatory school. 'Surely she can't manage Rosalind?'

'It was her great part. Happily you can play Rosalind at any age. Wish I could get old Ludlow to play Jaques. But he won't.' Ludlow was the company's veteran.

'Why not?'

'He played with Rokeby in the old days. I believe he's afraid she'll see he isn't the Grand Old Man he should be. He's a good chap, but proud. Of course he may have other reasons. You never know with Ludlow.'

The curtain was down on Act I.

Colvin took his leave and resumed his walk.

Shortly thereafter Colvin read about the Nethers Gala in the local evening paper ('this forgotten poet', as the writer helpfully phrased it), and found confirmation that Miss Rokeby was indeed to grace it ('the former London star'). In the same issue of the paper appeared an editorial to the effect that wide-spread disappointment would be caused by the news that the Hippodrome would not be offering a pantomime at Christmas in accordance with the custom of the town and district.

'She can't 'ardly stop 'ere, Mr Colvin,' said Mrs Royd, when Colvin, thinking to provide forewarning, showed her the news, as she lent a hand behind the saloon bar. 'This isn't the Cumberland. She'd get across the staff.'

'I believe she's quite elderly,' said Colvin soothingly.

'If she's elderly, she'll want special attention, and that's often just as bad.'

'After all, where she goes is mainly a problem for her, and perhaps Mr Malnik.'

'Well, there's nowhere else in town for her to stop, is there?' retorted Mrs Royd with fire. 'Not nowadays. She'll just 'ave to make do. We did for theatricals in the old days. Midgets once. Whole troupe of 'em.'

'I'm sure you'll make her very comfortable.'

'Can't see what she wants to come at all for, really. Not at Christmas.'

'Miss Rokeby needs no *reason* for her actions. What she does is sufficient in itself. You'll understand that, dear lady, when you meet her.' The speaker was a very small man, apparently of advanced years, white-haired, and with a brown sharp face, like a Levantine. The bar was full, and Colvin had not previously noticed him, although he was conspicuous enough, as he wore an overcoat with a fur collar and a scarf with a large black pin in the centre. 'I wonder if *I* could beg a room for a few nights,' he went on. 'I assure you I'm no trouble at all.'

'There's only Number Twelve A. It's not very comfortable,' replied Mrs Royd sharply.

'Of course you must leave room for Miss Rokeby.'

'Nine's for her. Though I haven't had a word from her.'

'I think she'll need two rooms. She has a companion.'

'I can clear out Greta's old room upstairs. If she's a friend of yours, you might ask her to let me know when she's coming.'

'Not a friend,' said the old man, smiling. 'But I follow her career.'

Mrs Royd brought a big red book from under the bar.

'What name, please?'

'Mr Superbus,' said the little old man. He had yellow, expressionless eyes.

'Will you register?'

Mr Superbus produced a gold pen, long and fat. His writing was so curvilinear that it seemed purely decorative, like a design for ornamental ironwork. Colvin noticed that he paused slightly at the 'Permanent Address' column, and then simply wrote (although it was difficult to be sure) what appeared to be 'North Africa'.

'Will you come this way?' said Mrs Royd, staring suspiciously at the newcomer's scrollwork in the visitor's book. Then, even more suspiciously, she added: 'What about luggage?'

Mr Superbus nodded gravely. 'I placed two bags outside.'

'Let's hope they're still there. They're rough in this town, you know.'

'I'm sure they're still there,' said Mr Superbus.

As he spoke the door opened suddenly and a customer almost fell into the bar. 'Sorry, Mrs Royd,' he said with a mildness which in the circumstances belied Mrs Royd's words. 'There's something on the step.'

'My fault, I'm afraid,' said Mr Superbus. 'I wonder—have you a porter?'

'The porter works evenings at the Hippodrome nowadays. Scene-shifting and that.'

'Perhaps I could help?' said Colvin.

On the step outside were what appeared to be two very large suitcases. When he tried to lift one of them, he understood what Mr Superbus had meant. It was remarkably heavy. He held back the bar door, letting in a cloud of cold air. 'Give me a hand, someone,' he said.

The customer who had almost fallen volunteered, and a short procession, led by Mrs Royd, set off along the little dark passage to Number Twelve A. Colvin was disconcerted when he realized that Twelve A was the room at the end of the passage, which had no number on its door and had never, he thought, been occupied since his arrival; the room, in fact, next to his.

'Better leave these on the floor,' said Colvin, dismissing the rickety luggage-stand.

'Thank you,' said Mr Superbus, transferring a coin to the man who had almost fallen. He did it like a conjuror unpalming something.

'I'll send Greta to make up the bed,' said Mrs Royd. 'Tea's at six.'

'At six?' said Mr Superbus, gently raising an eyebrow. 'Tea?' Then, when Mrs Royd and the man had gone, he clutched Colvin very hard on the upper part of his left arm. 'Tell me,' enquired Mr Superbus, 'are you in love with Miss Rokeby? I overheard you defending her against the impertinence of our hostess.'

Colvin considered for a moment.

'Why not admit it?' said Mr Superbus, gently raising the other eyebrow. He was still clutching Colvin's arm much too hard.

'I've never set eyes on Miss Rokeby.'

Mr Superbus let go. 'Young people nowadays have no imagination,' he said with a whinny, like a wild goat.

Colvin was not surprised when Mr Superbus did not appear for tea (pressed beef and chips that evening).

After tea Colvin, instead of going for a walk, wrote to his mother. But there was little to tell her, so that at the end of the letter he mentioned the arrival of Mr Superbus. 'There's a sort of sweet blossomy smell about him like a meadow,' he ended. 'I think he must use scent.'

When the letter was finished, Colvin started trying to construct tables of output from the lead and plumbago mines a century ago. The partitions between the bedrooms were thin, and he began to wonder about Mr Superbus's nocturnal habits.

He wondered from time to time until the time came for sleep; and wondered a bit also as he dressed the next morning and went to the bathroom to shave. For during the whole of this time no sound whatever had been heard from Number Twelve A, despite the thinness of the plywood partition; a circumstance which Colvin already thought curious when, during breakfast, he overheard Greta talking to Mrs Royd in the kitchen. 'I'm ever so sorry, Mrs Royd. I forgot about it with the crowd in the bar.' To which Mrs Royd simply replied: 'I wonder what 'e done about it. 'E could 'ardly do without sheets or blankets, and this December. Why didn't 'e *ask*?' And when Greta said, 'I suppose nothing ain't happened to him?' Colvin put down his porridge spoon and unobtrusively joined the party which went out to find out.

Mrs Royd knocked several times upon the door of Number Twelve A, but there was no answer. When they opened the door, the bed was bare as Colvin had seen it the evening before, and there was no sign at all of Mr Superbus except that his two big cases lay on the floor, one beside the other.

'What's he want to leave the window open like that for?' enquired Mrs Royd. She shut it with a crash. 'Someone will fall over those cases in the middle of the floor.'

Colvin bent down to slide the heavy cases under the bed. But the pair of them now moved at a touch.

Colvin picked one case up and shook it slightly. It emitted a muffled flapping sound, like a bat in a box. Colvin nearly spoke, but stopped himself, and stowed the cases, end on, under the unmade bed in silence.

'Make up the room, Greta,' said Mrs Royd. 'It's no use just standing about.' Colvin gathered that it was not altogether unknown for visitors to the Emancipation Hotel to be missing from their rooms all night.

But there was a further little mystery. Later that day in the bar, Colvin was accosted by the man who had helped to carry Mr Superbus's luggage.

'Look at that.' He displayed, rather furtively, something which lay in his hand.

It was a sovereign.

'He gave it me last night.'

'Can I see it?' It had been struck in Queen Victoria's reign, but gleamed like new.

'What d'you make of that?' asked the man.

'Not much,' replied Colvin, returning the pretty piece. 'But now I come to think of it, *you* can make about forty-five shillings.'

When this incident took place, Colvin was on his way to spend three or four nights in another town where lead and plumbago mining had formerly been carried on, and where he needed to consult an invaluable collection of old records which had been presented to the Public Library at the time the principal mining company went bankrupt.

On his return, he walked up the hill from the station through a thick mist, laden with coal dust and sticky smoke, and apparently in no way diminished by a bitter little wind, which chilled while hardly troubling to blow. There had been snow, and little archipelagos of slush remained on the pavements, through which the immense boots of the miners crashed noisily. The male population wore heavy mufflers and were unusually silent. Many of the women wore shawls over their heads in the manner of their grandmothers.

Mrs Royd was not in the bar, and Colvin hurried through it to his old room, where he put on a thick sweater before descending to tea. The only company consisted in two commercial travellers, sitting at the same table and eating through a heap of bread and margarine but saying nothing. Colvin wondered what had happened to Mr Superbus.

Greta entered as usual with a pot of strong tea and a plate of bread and margarine.

'Good evening, Mr Colvin. Enjoy your trip?'

'Yes, thank you, Greta. What's for tea?'

'Haddock and chips.' She drew a deep breath. 'Miss Rokeby's come... I don't think she'll care for haddock and chips do you, Mr Colvin?' Colvin looked up in surprise. He saw that Greta was trembling. Then he noticed that she was wearing a thin black dress, instead of her customary casual attire.

Colvin smiled up at her. 'I think you'd better put on something warm. It's getting colder every minute.'

But at that moment the door opened and Miss Rokeby entered.

Greta stood quite still, shivering all over, and simply staring at her. Everything about Greta made it clear that this was Miss Rokeby. Otherwise the situation was of a kind which brought to Colvin's mind the cliché about there being some mistake.

The woman who had come in was very small and slight. She had a triangular gazelle-like face, with very large dark eyes, and a mouth which went right across the lower tip of the triangle, making of her chin another, smaller triangle. She was dressed entirely in

136

black, with a high-necked black silk sweater, and wore long black earrings. Her short dark hair was dressed like that of a faun; and her thin white hands hung straight by her side in a posture resembling some Indian statuettes which Colvin recalled but could not place.

Greta walked towards her, and drew back a chair. She placed Miss Rokeby with her back to Colvin.

'Thank you. What can I eat?' Colvin was undecided whether Miss Rokeby's voice was high or low: it was like a bell beneath the ocean.

Greta was blushing. She stood, not looking at Miss Rokeby, but at the other side of the room, shivering and reddening. Then tears began to pour down her cheeks in a cataract. She dragged at a chair, made an unintelligible sound, and ran into the kitchen.

Miss Rokeby half turned in her seat, and stared after Greta. Colvin thought she looked quite as upset as Greta. Certainly she was very white. She might almost have been eighteen...

'Please don't mind. It's nerves, I think.' Colvin realized that his own voice was far from steady, and that he was beginning to blush also, he hoped only slightly.

Miss Rokeby had risen to her feet and was holding on to the back of her chair.

'I didn't say anything which could frighten her.'

It was necessary to come to the point, Colvin thought.

'Greta thinks the menu unworthy of the distinguished company.'

'What?' She turned and looked at Colvin. Then she smiled. 'Is that it?' She sat down again. 'What is it? Fish and chips?'

'Haddock. Yes.' Colvin smiled back, now full of confidence.

'Well. There it is.' Miss Rokeby made the prospect of haddock sound charming and gay. One of the commercial travellers offered to pour the other a fourth cup of tea. The odd little crisis was over.

But when Greta returned, her face seemed set and a trifle hostile. She had put on an ugly custard-coloured cardigan.

'It's haddock and chips.'

Miss Rokeby merely inclined her head, still smiling charmingly.

Before Colvin had finished, Miss Rokeby, with whom further conversation had been made difficult by the fact that she had been seated with her back to him, and by the torpid watchfulness of the commercial travellers, rose, bade him, 'Good evening', and left.

Colvin had not meant to go out again that evening, but curiosity continued to rise in him, and in the end he decided to clear his thoughts by a short walk, taking in the Hippodrome. Outside it had become even colder, the fog was thicker, the streets emptier.

Colvin found that the entrance to the Hippodrome had been transformed. From frieze to floor, the walls were covered with large photographs. The photographs were not framed, but merely mounted on big sheets of pasteboard. They seemed to be all the same size. Colvin saw at once that they were all portraits of Miss Rokeby.

The entrance hall was filled with fog, but the lighting within had been greatly reinforced since Colvin's last visit. Tonight the effect was mistily dazzling. Colvin began to examine the photographs. They depicted Miss Rokeby in the widest variety of costumes and make-up, although in no case was the name given of the play or character. In some Colvin could not see how he recognized her at all. In all she was alone. The number of the photographs, their uniformity of presentation, the bright swimming lights, the emptiness of the place (for the Box Office had shut) combined to make Colvin feel that he was dreaming. He put his hands before his eyes, inflamed by the glare and the fog. When he looked again, it was as if all the

Miss Rokebys had been so placed that their gaze converged upon the spot where he stood. He closed his eyes tightly and began to feel his way to the door and the dimness of the street outside. Then there was a flutter of applause behind him; the evening's audience began to straggle out, grumbling at the weather; and Malnik was saying 'Hullo, old man. Nice to see you.'

Colvin gesticulated uncertainly. 'Did she bring them all with her?'

'Not a bit of it, old man. Millie found them when she opened up.'

'Where did she find them?'

'Just lying on the floor. In two whacking great parcels. Rokeby's agent, I suppose, though she appeared not to have one. Blest if I know, really. I myself could hardly shift one of the parcels, let alone two.'

Colvin felt rather frightened for a moment; but he only said: 'How do you like her?'

'Tell you when she arrives.'

'She's arrived.'

Malnik stared.

'Come back with me and see for yourself.'

Malnik seized Colvin's elbow. 'What's she look like?'

'Might be any age.'

All the time Malnik was bidding good night to patrons, trying to appease their indignation at being brought out on such a night.

Suddenly the lights went, leaving only a pilot. It illumined a photograph of Miss Rokeby holding a skull.

'Let's go,' said Malnik. 'Lock up, Frank, will you?'

'You'll need a coat,' said Colvin.

'Lend me your coat, Frank.'

*

On the short cold walk to the Emancipation Hotel, Malnik said little. Colvin supposed that he was planning the encounter before him. Colvin did ask him whether he had ever heard of a Mr Superbus, but he hadn't.

Mrs Royd was, it seemed, in a thoroughly bad temper. To Colvin it appeared that she had been drinking; and that she was one whom drink soured rather than mellowed. 'I've got no one to send,' she snapped. 'You can go up yourself, if you like. Mr Colvin knows the way.' There was a roaring fire in the bar, which after the cold outside seemed very overheated.

Outside Number Nine, Colvin paused before knocking. Immediately he was glad he had done so, because inside were voices speaking very softly. All the evening he had been remembering Mr Superbus's reference to a 'companion'.

In dumb-show he tried to convey the situation to Malnik, who peered at his efforts with a professional's dismissal of the amateur. Then Malnik produced a pocket-book, wrote in it, and tore out the page, which he thrust under Miss Rokeby's door. Having done this, he prepared to return with Colvin to the bar, and await a reply. Before they had taken three steps, however, the door was open, and Miss Rokeby was inviting them in.

To Colvin she said, 'We've met already', though without enquiring his name.

Colvin felt gratified; and at least equally pleased when he saw that the fourth person in the room was a tall, frail-looking girl with long fair hair drawn back into a tight bun. It was not the sort of companion he had surmised.

'This is Myrrha. We're never apart.'

Myrrha smiled slightly, said nothing, and sat down again. Colvin thought she looked positively wasted. Doubtless by reason of the cold, she wore heavy tweeds, which went oddly with her air of fragility.

'How well do you know the play?' asked Malnik at the earliest possible moment.

'Well enough not to play in it.' Colvin saw Malnik turn grey. 'Since you've got me here, I'll play Rosalind. The rest was lies. Do you know,' she went on, addressing Colvin, 'that this man tried to trick me? You're not in the theatre, are you?'

Colvin, feeling embarrassed, smiled and shook his head.

'*Cornelia* is a masterpiece,' said Malnik furiously. 'Nethers was a genius.'

Miss Rokeby simply said 'Was' very softly, and seated herself on the arms of Myrrha's armchair, the only one in the room. It was set before the old-fashioned gas-fire.

'It's announced. Everyone's waiting for it. People are coming from London. They're even coming from Cambridge.' Myrrha turned away her head from Malnik's wrath.

'I was told—Another English Classic. Not an out-pouring by little Jack Nethers. I won't do it.'

'*As You Like It* is only a fill-up. What more is it ever? *Cornelia* is the whole point of the Gala. Nethers was *born* in this town. Don't you understand?'

Malnik was so much in earnest that Colvin felt sorry for him. But even Colvin doubted whether Malnik's was the best way to deal with Miss Rokeby.

'Please play for me. Please.'

'Rosalind only.' Miss Rokeby was swinging her legs. They were young and lovely. There was more than one thing about this interview which Colvin did not care for.

'We'll talk it over in my office tomorrow.' Colvin identified this as a customary admission of defeat.

'This is a horrid place, isn't it?' said Miss Rokeby conversationally to Colvin.

'I'm used to it,' said Colvin, smiling. 'Mrs Royd has her softer side.'

'She's put poor Myrrha in a cupboard.'

Colvin remembered about Greta's old room upstairs.

'Perhaps she'd like to change rooms with me? I've been away and haven't even unpacked. It would be easy.'

'How kind you are! To that silly little girl! To me! And now to Myrrha! May I see?'

'Of course.'

Colvin took her into the passage. It seemed obvious that Myrrha would come also, but she did not. Apparently she left it to Miss Rokeby to dispose of her. Malnik sulked behind also.

Colvin opened the door of his room and switched on the light. Lying on his bed and looking very foolish was his copy of Bull's *Graphite and Its Uses*. He glanced round for Miss Rokeby. Then for the second time that evening, he felt frightened.

Miss Rokeby was standing in the ill-lit passage, just outside his doorway. It was unpleasantly apparent that she was terrified. Formerly pale, she was now quite white. Her hands were clenched, and she was breathing unnaturally deeply. Her big eyes were half shut, and to Colvin it seemed that it was something she *smelt* which was frightening her. This impression was so strong that he sniffed the chilly air himself once or twice, unavailingly. Then he stepped forward, and his arms were around Miss Rokeby, who was palpably about to faint. Immediately Miss Rokeby was in his arms, such emotion swept through him as he had never before known. For what seemed a long moment, he was lost in the wonder of it. Then he was recalled by something which frightened him more than anything else, though for less reason. There was a sharp sound from Number Twelve A. Mr Superbus must have returned.

Colvin supported Miss Rokeby back to Number Nine. Upon catching sight of her, Myrrha gave a small but jarring cry, and helped her on to the bed.

'It's my heart,' said Miss Rokeby. 'My absurd heart.'

Malnik now looked more black than grey. 'Shall we send for a doctor?' he enquired, hardly troubling to mask the sarcasm.

Miss Rokeby shook her head once. It was the sibling gesture to her nod.

'Please don't trouble about moving,' she said to Colvin.

Colvin, full of confusion, looked at Myrrha, who was being resourceful with smelling-salts.

'Good night,' said Miss Rokeby, softly but firmly. And as Colvin followed Malnik out of the room, she touched his hand.

Colvin passed the night almost without sleep, which was another new experience for him. A conflict of feelings about Miss Rokeby, all of them strong, was one reason for insomnia: another was the sequence of sounds from Number Twelve A. Mr Superbus seemed to spend the night in moving things about and talking to himself. At first it sounded as if he were rearranging all the furniture in his room. Then there was a period, which seemed to Colvin timeless, during which the only noise was of low and unintelligible mutterings, by no means continuous, but broken by periods of silence and then resumed as before just as Colvin was beginning to hope that all was over. Colvin wondered whether Mr Superbus was saying his prayers. Ultimately the banging about recommenced. Presumably Mr Superbus was still dissatisfied with the arrangement of the furniture; or perhaps was returning it to its original dispositions. Then Colvin heard the sash-window thrown sharply open. He remembered the sound from the occasion when Mrs Royd had sharply shut it. After that silence continued. In the end Colvin turned on the light and looked at his watch. It had stopped.

At breakfast, Colvin asked when Mr Superbus was expected down. 'He doesn't come down,' replied Greta. 'They say he has all his meals out.'

Colvin understood that rehearsals began that day, but Malnik had always demurred at outsiders being present. Now, moreover, he felt that Colvin had seen him at an unfavourable moment, so that his cordiality was much abated. The next two weeks, in fact, were to Colvin heavy with anti-climax. He saw Miss Rokeby only at the evening meal, which, however, she was undeniably in process of converting from tea to dinner, by expending charm, will-power, and cash. Colvin participated in this improvement, as did even such few of the endless commercial travellers as wished to do so; and from time to time Miss Rokeby exchanged a few pleasant, generalities with him, though she did not ask him to sit at her table, nor did he, being a shy man, dare to invite her. Myrrha never appeared at all; and when on one occasion Colvin referred to her interrogatively, Miss Rokeby simply said, 'She pines, poor lamb,' and plainly wished to say nothing more. Colvin remembered Myrrha's wasted appearance, and concluded that she must be an invalid. He wondered if he should again offer to change rooms. After that single disturbed night, he had heard no more of Mr Superbus. But from Mrs Royd he had gathered that Mr Superbus had settled for several weeks in advance. Indeed, for the first time in years the Emancipation Hotel was doing good business.

It continued as cold as ever during all the time Miss Rokeby remained in the town, with repeated little snow storms every time the streets began to clear. The miners would stamp as they entered the bar until they seemed likely to go through to the cellar beneath; and all the commercial travellers caught colds. The two local papers, morning and evening, continued their efforts to set people against Malnik's now diminished Gala. When *Cornelia* was no longer offered, the two editors pointed out (erroneously, Colvin felt) that even now it was not too late for a pantomime: but Malnik seemed to have succeeded in persuading Miss Rokeby to reinforce *As You Like It* with a piece entitled *A Scrap of Paper* which Colvin had never heard of, but which an elderly local citizen whom the papers always consulted upon matters theatrical described as 'very old-fashioned'. Malnik caused further comment by proposing to open on Christmas Eve, when the unfailing tradition had been Boxing Night.

The final week of rehearsal was marred by an exceedingly distressing incident. It happened on the Tuesday. Coming in that morning from a cold visit to the Technical Institute Library, Colvin found in the stuffy little saloon bar a number of the Tabard Players. The Players usually patronized an establishment nearer to the Hippodrome; and the fact that the present occasion was out of the ordinary was emphasized by the demeanour of the group, who were clustered together and talking in low, serious voices. Colvin knew none of the players at all well, but the group looked so distraught that, partly from curiosity and partly from compassion, he ventured to enquire of one of them, a middle-aged actor named Shillitoe to whom Malnik had introduced him, what was the matter. After a short silence, the group seemed collectively to decide upon accepting Colvin among them, and all began to enlighten him in short strained bursts of over-eloquence. Some of the references were not wholly clear to Colvin, but the substance of the story was simple.

Colvin gathered that when the Tabard Players took possession of the Hippodrome, Malnik had been warned that the 'grid' above the stage was undependable, and that scenery should not be 'flown' from it. This restriction had caused grumbling, but had been complied with until, during a rehearsal of *A Scrap of Paper*, the producer had rebelled and asked Malnik for authority to use the grid. Malnik had agreed; and two stage-hands began gingerly to pull on some of the dusty lines which disappeared into the almost complete darkness far above. Before long one of them had cried out that there was 'something up there already'. At these words, Colvin was told, everyone in the theatre fell silent. The stage-hand went on paying out line, but the stage was so ample and the grid so high that an appreciable time passed before the object came slowly into view.

The narrators stopped, and there was a silence which Colvin felt must have been like the silence in the theatre. Then Shillitoe resumed: 'It was poor old Ludlow's body. He'd hanged himself right up under the grid. Eighty feet above the floor of the stage. Some time ago, too. He wasn't in the Christmas plays, you know. Or in this week's play. We all thought he'd gone home.'

Colvin learnt that the producer had fainted right away; and, upon tactful enquiry, that Miss Rokeby had fortunately not been called for that particular rehearsal.

On the first two Sundays after her arrival, Miss Rokeby had been no more in evidence than on any other day; but on the morning of the third Sunday Colvin was taking one of his resolute lonely walks across the windy fells which surrounded the town when he saw her walking ahead of him through the snow. The snow lay only an inch or two deep upon the hillside ledge along which the path ran; and Colvin had been wondering for some time about the small footsteps which preceded him. It was the first time he had seen Miss Rokeby outside the Emancipation Hotel, but he had no doubt that it was she he saw, and his heart turned over at the sight. He hesitated; then walked faster, and soon had overtaken her. As he drew near, she stopped, turned, and faced him. Then, when she saw who it was, she seemed unsurprised. She wore a fur coat with a collar which reached almost to the tip of her nose; a fur hat; and elegant boots which laced to the knee.

'I'm glad to have a companion,' she said gravely, sending Colvin's thought to her other odd companion. 'I suppose you know all these paths well?'

'I come up here often to look for lead-workings. I'm writing a dull book on lead and plumbago mining.'

'I don't see any mines up here.' She looked around with an air of grave bewilderment.

'Lead mines aren't like coal mines. They're simply passages in hillsides.'

'What do you do when you find them?'

'I mark them on a large-scale map. Sometimes I go down them.'

'Don't the miners object?'

'There are no miners.'

A shadow crossed her face.

'I mean, not any longer. We don't mine lead any more.'

'Don't we? Why not?'

'That's a complicated story.'

She nodded. 'Will you take me down a mine?'

'I don't think you'd like it. The passages are usually both narrow and low. One of the reasons why the industry's come to an end is that people would no longer work in them. Besides, now the mines are disused, they're often dangerous.'

She laughed. It was the first time he had ever heard her do so. 'Come on.' She took hold of his arm. 'Or aren't there any mines on this particular hillside?' She looked as concerned as a child.

'There's one about a hundred feet above our heads. But there's nothing to see. Only darkness.'

'Only *darkness*,' cried Miss Rokeby. She implied that no reasonable person could want more. 'But you don't go down all these passages only to see darkness?'

'I take a flashlight.'

'Have you got it now?'

'Yes.' Colvin never went to the fells without it.

'Then that will look after *you*. Where's the mine? Conduct me.'

They began to scramble together up the steep snow-covered slope. Colvin knew all the workings round here; and soon they were in the entry.

'You see,' said Colvin. 'There's not even room to stand, and a fat person couldn't get in at all. You'll ruin your coat.'

'I'm not a fat person.' There was a small excited patch in each of her cheeks. 'But you'd better go first.'

Colvin knew that this particular working consisted simply in a long passage, following the vein of lead. He had been to the end of it more than once. He turned on his flashlight. 'I assure you, there's nothing to see,' he said. And in he went.

148

Colvin perceived that Miss Rokeby seemed indeed to pass along the adit without even stooping or damaging her fur hat. She insisted on going as far as possible, although near the end Colvin made a quite strenuous effort to persuade her to let them return.

'What's that?' enquired Miss Rokeby when they had none the less reached the extremity of the passage.

'It's a big fault in the limestone. A sort of cave. The miners chucked their débris down it.'

'Is it deep?'

'Some of these faults are supposed to be bottomless.'

She took the light from his hand, and, squatting down on the brink of the hole, flashed it round the depths below.

'Careful,' cried Colvin. 'You're on loose shale. It could easily slip.' He tried to drag her back. The only result was that she dropped the flashlight, which went tumbling down the great hole like a meteor, until after many seconds they heard a faint crash. They were in complete darkness.

'I'm sorry,' said Miss Rokeby's voice. 'But you did push me.'

Trying not to fall down the hole, Colvin began to grope his way back. Suddenly he had thought of Malnik, and the irresponsibility of the proceedings upon which he was engaged appalled him. He begged Miss Rokeby to go slowly, test every step, and mind her head; but her unconcern seemed complete. Colvin tripped and toiled along for an endless period of time, with Miss Rokeby always close behind him, calm, sure of foot, and unflagging. As far into the earth as this, it was both warm and stuffy. Colvin began to fear that bad air might overcome them, forced as they were to creep so laboriously and interminably. He broke out in heavy perspiration.

Suddenly he knew that he would have to stop. He could not even pretend that it was out of consideration for Miss Rokeby. He subsided upon the floor of the passage and she seated herself near him, oblivious of her costly clothes. The blackness was still complete.

'Don't feel unworthy,' said Miss Rokeby softly. 'And don't feel frightened. There's no need. We shall get out.'

Curiously enough, the more she said, the worse Colvin felt. The strange antecedents to this misadventure were with him; and, even more so, Miss Rokeby's whole fantastic background. He had to force his spine against the stone wall of the passage if he were not to give way to panic utterly and leap up screaming. Normal speech was impossible.

'Is it me you are frightened of?' asked Miss Rokeby, with dreadful percipience.

Colvin was less than ever able to speak.

'Would you like to know more about me?'

Colvin was shaking his head in the dark.

'If you'll promise not to tell anyone else.'

But, in fact, she was like a child, unable to contain her secret.

'I'm sure you won't tell anyone else... It's my helper. He's the queer one. Not me.'

Now that the truth was spoken Colvin felt a little better. 'Yes,' he said in a low, shaken voice, 'I know.'

'Oh, you know... I don't see him or—' she paused—'or encounter him, often for years at a time. Years.'

'But you encountered him the other night?'

He could feel her shudder. 'Yes... You've seen him?'

'Very briefly... How did you... encounter him first?'

'It was years ago. Have you any idea how many years?'

'I think so.'

Then she said something which Colvin never really understood; not even later, in his dreams of her. 'You know I'm not here at all, really. Myrrha's me. That's why she's called Myrrha. That's how I act.'

'How?' said Colvin. There was little else to say.

'My helper took my own personality out of me. Like taking a nerve out of a tooth. Myrrha's my personality.'

'Do you mean your soul?' asked Colvin.

'Artists don't have souls,' said Miss Rokeby. 'Personality's the word... I'm anybody's personality. Or everybody's. And when I lost my personality, I stopped growing older. Of course I have to look after Myrrha, because if anything happened to Myrrha—well, you do see,' she continued.

'But Myrrha looks as young as you do.'

'That's what she *looks*.'

Colvin remembered Myrrha's wasted face.

'But how can you live without a personality? Besides,' added Colvin, 'you seem to me to have a very strong personality.'

'I have a mask for every occasion.'

It was only the utter blackness, Colvin felt, which made this impossible conversation possible.

'What do you do in exchange? I suppose you must repay your helper in some way?'

'I suppose I must... I've never found out what way it is.'

'What else does your helper do for you?'

'He smooths my path. Rids me of people who want to hurt me. He rid me of little Jack Nethers. Jack was mad, you know. You can see it even in his photograph.'

'Did he rid you of this wretched man Ludlow?'

'I don't know. You see, I can't remember Ludlow. I think he often rids me of people that I don't know want to hurt me.'

Colvin considered.

'Can you be rid of him?'

'I've never really tried.'

'Don't you *want* to be rid of him?'

'I don't know. He frightens me terribly whenever I come near him, but otherwise... I don't know... But for him I should never have been down a lead mine.'

'How many people know all this?' asked Colvin after a pause.

'Not many. I only told you because I wanted you to stop being frightened.'

As she spoke the passage was filled with a strange sound. Then they were illumined with icy December sunshine. Colvin perceived that they were almost at the entry to the working, and supposed that the portal must have been temporarily blocked by a miniature avalanche of melting snow. Even now there was, in fact, only a comparatively small hole, through which they would have to scramble.

'I told you we'd get out,' said Miss Rokeby. 'Other people haven't believed a word I said. But now *you'll* believe me.'

Not the least strange thing was the matter-of-fact manner in which, all the way back, Miss Rokeby questioned Colvin about his researches into lead and plumbago mining, with occasionally, on the perimeter of their talk, flattering enquiries about himself; although equally strange, Colvin considered, was the matter-of-fact manner in which he answered her. Before they were back in the town he was wondering how much of what she had said in the darkness of the mine had been meant only figuratively; and after that he wondered whether Miss Rokeby had not used the circumstances to initiate an imaginative and ingenious boutade. After all, he reflected, she was an actress. Colvin's hypothesis was, if anything, confirmed when at their parting she held his hand for a moment and said: 'Remember! *No one.*'

But he resolved to question Mrs Royd in a business-like way about Mr Superbus. An opportunity arose when he encountered her after luncheon (at which Miss Rokeby had not made an appearance), reading *The People* before the fire in the saloon bar. The bar had just closed, and it was, Mrs Royd explained, the only warm spot in the house. In fact it was, as usual, hot as a kiln.

'Couldn't say, I'm sure,' replied Mrs Royd to Colvin's firm enquiry, and implying that it was neither her business nor his. 'Anyway, 'e's gone. Went last Tuesday. Didn't you notice, with 'im sleeping next to you?'

After the death of poor Ludlow (the almost inevitable verdict was suicide while of unsound mind), it was as if the papers felt embarrassed about continuing to carp at Malnik's plans; and by the opening night the editors seemed ready to extend the Christmas spirit even to Shakespeare. Colvin had planned to spend Christmas with his mother; but when he learned that Malnik's first night was to be on Christmas Eve, had been unable to resist deferring his departure until after it, despite the perils of a long and intricate railway journey on Christmas Day. With Miss Rokeby, however, he now felt entirely unsure of himself.

On Christmas Eve the town seemed full of merriment. Colvin was surprised at the frankness of the general rejoicing. The shops, as is usual in industrial districts, had long been off-setting the general drabness with drifts of Christmas cards and whirlpools of tinsel. Now every home seemed to be decorated and all the shops to be proclaiming bonus distributions and bumper share-outs. Even the queues, which were a prominent feature of these celebrations, looked more sanguine, Colvin noticed, when he stood in one of them for about half an hour in order to send Miss Rokeby some flowers, as he felt the occasion demanded. By the time he set out for the Hippodrome, the more domestically-minded citizens were everywhere quietly toiling at preparations for the morrow's revels; but a wilder minority, rebellious or homeless, were inaugurating such a carouse at the Emancipation Hotel as really to startle the comparatively retiring Colvin. He suspected that some of the bibbers must be Irish.

Sleet was slowly descending as Colvin stepped out of the sweltering bar in order to walk to the Hippodrome. A spot of it sailed gently into the back of his neck, chilling him in a moment. But notwithstanding the weather, notwithstanding the claims of the season and the former attitude of the Press, there was a crowd outside the Hippodrome such as Colvin had never previously seen there. To his great surprise, some of the audience were in evening dress; many of them had expensive cars, and one party, it appeared, had come in a closed carriage with two flashing black horses. There was such a concourse at the doors that Colvin had to stand a long time in the slowly falling sleet before he was able to join the throng which forced its way, like icing on to a cake, between the countless glittering photographs of beautiful Miss Rokeby. The average age of the audience, Colvin observed, seemed very advanced, and especially of that section of it which was in evening dress. Elderly white-haired men with large noses and carnations in their buttonholes spoke in elegant Edwardian voices to the witch-like ladies on their arms, most of whom wore hot-house gardenias.

Inside, however, the huge and golden Hippodrome looked as it was intended to look when it was still named the Grand Opera House. From his gangway seat in the stalls Colvin looked backwards and upwards at the gilded satyrs and bacchantes who wantoned on the dress-circle balustrade; and at the venerable and orchidaceous figures who peered above them. The small orchestra was frenziedly playing selections from *L'Étoile du Nord*. In the gallery distant figures, unable to find seats, were standing watchfully. Even the many boxes, little used and dusty, were filling up. Colvin could only speculate how this gratifying assembly had been collected. But then he was on his feet for the National Anthem, and the faded crimson and gold curtain, made deceivingly splendid by the footlights, was about to rise.

The play began, and then: 'Dear Celia, I show more mirth than I am mistress of, and would you yet I were merrier? Unless you could teach me to forget a banished father, you must not learn me how to remember any extraordinary pleasure.'

Colvin realized that in his heart he had expected Miss Rokeby to be good, to be moving, to be lovely; but the revelation he now had was something he could never have expected because he could never have imagined it; and before the conclusion of Rosalind's first scene in boy's attire in the Forest, he was wholly and terribly bewitched.

No one coughed, no one rustled, no one moved. To Colvin, it seemed as if Miss Rokeby's magic had strangely enchanted the normally journeyman Tabard Players into miracles of judgment. Plainly her spell was on the audience also; so that when the lights came up for the interval, Colvin found that his eyes were streaming, and felt not chagrin, but pride.

The interval was an uproar. Even the bells of fire-engines pounding through the wintry night outside could hardly be heard above the din. People spoke freely to unknown neighbours, groping to express forgotten emotions. 'What a prelude to Christmas!' everyone said. Malnik was proved right in one thing.

During the second half, Colvin, failing of interest in Sir Oliver Martext's scene, let his eyes wander round the auditorium. He noticed that the nearest dress-circle box, previously unoccupied, appeared to be unoccupied no longer. A hand, which, being only just above him, he could see was gnarled and hirsute, was tightly gripping the box's red velvet curtain. Later in the scene between Silvius and Phebe (Miss Rokeby having come and gone meanwhile), the hand was still there, and still gripping tightly; as it was (after Rosalind's big scene with Orlando) during the Forester's song. At the beginning of Act V, there was a rush of feet down the gangway, and someone was crouching by Colvin's seat. It was Greta. 'Mr Colvin! There's been a fire. Miss Rokeby's friend jumped out of the window. She's terribly hurt. Will you tell Miss Rokeby?'

'The play's nearly over,' said Colvin. 'Wait for me at the back.' Greta withdrew, whimpering.

After Rosalind's Epilogue the tumult was millennial. Miss Rokeby, in Rosalind's white dress, stood for many seconds not bowing but quite still and unsmiling, with her hands by her sides as Colvin had first seen her. Then as the curtain rose and revealed the rest of the company, she began slowly to walk backwards upstage. Door-keepers and even stage-hands, spruced up for the purpose, began to bring armfuls upon armfuls of flowers, until there was a heap, a mountain of them in the centre of the stage, so high that it concealed Miss Rokeby's figure from the audience. Suddenly a bouquet flew through the air from the dress-circle box. It landed at the very front of the heap. It was a hideous dusty laurel wreath, adorned with an immense and somewhat tasteless purple bow. The audience were yelling for Miss Rokeby like Dionysians; and the company, flagging from unaccustomed emotional expenditure, and plainly much scared, were looking for her; but in the end the stage-manager had to lower the Safety Curtain and give orders that the house be cleared.

Back at the Emancipation Hotel, Colvin, although he had little title, asked to see the body.

'You wouldn't ever recognize her,' said Mrs Royd. Colvin did not pursue the matter.

The snow, falling ever more thickly, had now hearsed the town in silence.

'She didn't 'ave to do it,' wailed on Mrs Royd. 'The brigade had the flames under control. And tomorrow Christmas Day!'

A PHANTOM LOVER
and Other Dark Tales by Vernon Lee

ISBN 978 0 7123 5381 6 · 288 pages

Be prepared to enter a unique and unsettling world in this new collection of dark fantasies from the unparalleled imagination of Vernon Lee. These are tales of lonely souls possessed by recurring tragedies of the past, holy sanctuaries disrupted by unruly pagan forces and aspiring youths enthralled and consumed by the undying art of their ancestors.

EVIL ROOTS
Killer Tales of the Botanical Gothic

ISBN 978 0 7123 5229 1 · 288 pages

Strangling vines and meat-hungry flora fill this unruly garden of strange stories, selected for their significance as the seeds of the villainous (or perhaps just misunderstood) 'killer plant' in fiction, film and video games.

Step within to marvel at Charlotte Perkins Gilman's giant wisteria and H. G. Wells' hungry orchid; hear the calls of the ethereal women of the wood, and the frightful drone of the moaning lily; and do tread carefully around E. Nesbit's wandering creepers...

CRAWLING HORROR
Creeping Tales of the Insect Weird

ISBN 978 0 7123 5349 6 · 320 pages

A brush with a killer hornet upends a reverend's life. A moth wreaks a strange vengeance on an entomologist. Bees deliver a supernatural dilemma to a mother-to-be. This new anthology offers a broad range of stories from the long history of insect literature, where six-legged beasts play many roles from lethal enemies to ethereal messengers.

RANDALLS ROUND
Nine Nightmares by Eleanor Scott

ISBN 978 0 7123 5405 9 · 240 pages

Randalls Round has long been revered by devotees of the weird tale. First published in 1929, its stories of ritualistic folk horror and M. R. James-inspired accounts of ancient forces terrorising humanity are thoroughly deserving of wider recognition. This collection includes a new introduction exploring Eleanor Scott's impact on weird and folk horror fiction, and two chilling stories by N. Dennett – speculated to be another of the author's pseudonyms.

WEIRD WOODS
Tales from the Haunted Forests of Britain

ISBN 978 0 7123 5342 7 · 240 pages

Woods play a crucial and recurring role in horror, fantasy, the gothic and the weird. They are places in which strange things happen, where it is easy to lose your way. Supernatural creatures thrive in the thickets. Trees reach into underworlds of pagan myth and magic. Forests are full of ghosts.

Lining the path through this realm of folklore and fear are twelve stories from across Britain, celebrating the enduring power of our natural spaces to enthral and terrorise our senses.

CHILL TIDINGS
Dark Tales of the Christmas Season

ISBN 978 0 7123 5323 6 · 224 pages

The gifts are unwrapped, the feast has been consumed and the fire is well fed – but the ghosts are still hungry. The ghosts are at the door. With classic tales from Algernon Blackwood, Elizabeth Bowen, Charlotte Riddell and L. P. Hartley jostling with rare pieces from the sleeping periodicals and literary magazines of the British Library collections, it's time to open the door and let the real festivities begin.

DOORWAY TO DILEMMA
Bewildering Tales of Dark Fantasy

ISBN 978 0 7123 5263 5 · 304 pages

Welcome to the realm of Dark Fantasy, where the weird prevails and accounts of unanswerable dilemma find their home. Gathered within these pages are twisted yarns, encounters with logic-defying creatures and nightmarish fables certain to perplex and beguile.

So join us as we journey across the threshold, deep into the British Library's vaults where nineteen deliciously dark and totally dumbfounding stories await. These tales, plucked from long-lost literary magazines and anthologies spring to life again to embody this most mesmerising of genres.

SUNLESS SOLSTICE
Strange Christmas Tales for the Longest Nights

ISBN 978 0 7123 5410 3 · 288 pages

Strange things happen on the dark wintry nights of December. Welcome to a new collection of haunting Christmas tales, ranging from traditional Victorian chillers to weird and uncanny episodes by twentieth-century horror masters including Daphne du Maurier and Robert Aickman.

Lurking in the blizzard are menacing cat spirits, vengeful trees, malignant forces on the mountainside and a skater skirting the line between the mortal and spiritual realms. Wrap up warm – and prepare for the longest nights of all.

POLAR HORRORS
Strange Tales from the World's Ends

ISBN 978 0 7123 5442 4 · 352 pages

From lurid Arctic narratives of life amongst polar bears to tales of ghostly visitations within the wind-blown wilds of the southern continent, this new collection uncovers a wealth of neglected material from this niche of literature obsessed with the limits of human experience.

Featuring tales rife with aliens, twisted science and madness spanning from 1837–1946, this anthology also includes a gem of twenty-first century Arctic horror to trace the enduring lure of these sublime and uncanny spaces at the ends of the Earth.

HAUNTERS AT THE HEARTH
Eerie Tales for Christmas Nights

ISBN 978 0 7123 5427 1 · 320 pages

When the boundary between the mundane and the unearthly is ever so thin—ushering in a new throng of revenants, demons, spectres and shades drawn to the glow of the Christmas hearth.

Included within are eighteen classic stories ranging from 1864 to 1974, with vintage Victorian chillers nestled alongside unsettling modern pieces from L. P. Hartley and Mildred Clingerman; lost tales from rare anthologies and periodicals; weird episodes from unexpected authors such as Winston Graham and D. H. Lawrence; stories simmering with a twisted humour from Elizabeth Bowen and Celia Fremlin and many more haunting seasonal treats.

SPECTRAL SOUNDS
Unquiet Tales of Acoustic Weird

ISBN 978 0 7123 5417 2 · 320 pages

Gathered here are fourteen tales which resonate with the unique note of fear struck by weird happenings experienced through the aural sense.

Divided into four sections exploring noises from invisible presences, ghostly voices, possessed technology and the power of extreme levels of sound or silence, this collection pulses with pioneering pieces from B. M. Croker, Algernon Blackwood, Edith Wharton and M. P. Shiel alongside haunting obscurities from the British Library collections.

THE HORNED GOD
Weird Tales of the Great God Pan

ISBN 978 0 7123 5496 7 · 320 pages

In 1894, Arthur Machen's landmark novella *The Great God Pan* was published, sparking the resurgence of the pagan goat god. Writers of the late-nineteenth to mid-twentieth centuries, such as Oscar Wilde, E. M. Forster and Margery Lawrence, took the god's rebellious influence as inspiration to spin beguiling tales.

Assembling ten tales and six poems – along with Machen's novella – from the boom years of Pan-centric literature, this new collection revels in themes of queer awakening, transgression against societal bonds and the bewitching power of the wild as it explores a rapturous and culturally significant chapter in the history of weird fiction.

OUR HAUNTED SHORES
Tales from the Coasts of the British Isles

ISBN 978 0 7123 5421 9 · 320 pages

From foreboding cliffs and lonely lighthouses to rumbling shingles and silted estuaries, the coasts of the British Isles have stoked the imaginations of storytellers for millennia, lending a rich literary significance to these spaces between land and sea.

This new collection of fifteen short stories, six folk tales and four poems ranging from 1789 to 1933 offers a chilling literary tour of the coasts of Great Britain, Ireland and the Isle of Man, including haunting pieces by Frances Hodgson Burnett, Bram Stoker and Charlotte Riddell.

THE GHOST SLAYERS
Thrilling Tales of Occult Detection

ISBN 978 0 7123 5416 5 · 288 pages

Occult or psychic detective tales have been chilling readers since the 1800s. This beguiling subgenre follows specialists in occult lore – often with years of arcane training – investigating supernatural occurrences and pitting their wits against bizarre, terrifying and deadly forces.

This new collection assembles nine unnerving cases, including the strange encounters of prominent psychic detectives such as Carnacki, the Ghost Finder and Dr. Silence along with lesser-known, rarely reprinted episodes investigated by the likes of Flaxman Low, Cosmo Thor, Aylmer Vance and Mesmer Milann.

SHADOWS ON THE WALL
Dark Tales by Mary E. Wilkins Freeman

ISBN 978 0 7123 5406 6 · 320 pages

The disquieting tales of Mary E. Wilkins Freeman explore a world of contrast, where the supernatural erupts out of authentically drawn portraits of New England life. This is a world of witchcraft, secrecy, domestic spaces turned uncanny and ancestral vengeances inflicted upon the unfortunates of the present.

Collecting the best of the author's strange tales – including 'The White Shawl', which was unpublished during her lifetime – this volume casts a light on an underappreciated contributor to weird fiction and the shadowy corners of a dark imagination.

THE NIGHT WIRE
and Other Tales of Weird Media

ISBN 978 0 7123 5411 0 · 320 pages

The ground-breaking new technologies of the nineteenth and twentieth centuries delivered their users into a world of unfathomable miracles and fresh nightmares – a world in which pioneers of weird fiction gave expression to the anxieties at the heart of seemingly limitless communication and the capturing of images beyond the human eye.

This collection presents seventeen tales of haunted and uncanny media from a range of writers inspired by its ghastly potential, including Marjorie Bowen, H. Russell Wakefield, Mary Treadgold and J. B. Priestley.

HEAVY WEATHER
Tempestuous Tales of Stranger Climes

ISBN 978 0 7123 5358 8 · 336 pages

From the flood myths of Babylon, the Mahabharata and the Bible, to twentieth-century psychological storms, this foray into troubled waters, malicious heat waves, vengeful winters, hurricanes and hailstones, offers the perfect read on a rainy day – or night.

Featuring tales of unearthly climatic phenomena from some of the finest writers in the English language including Algernon Blackwood, Herman Melville, William Hope Hodgson, Edgar Allan Poe and more, this collection of weird tales will delight and disturb.

DANGEROUS DIMENSIONS
Mind-bending Tales of the Mathematical Weird

ISBN 978 0 7123 5368 7 · 336 pages

Here, unimaginable terrors lurk in hitherto unknown mirror dimensions, calamities in ultra-space threaten to wipe clean all evidence of our universe and experiments in non-Euclidean geometry lead to sickening consequences.

In twelve speculative tales of our universe's mathematics and physics gone awry, this new anthology presents an abundance of curiosities –and terrors – with stories from Jorge Luis Borges, Miriam Allen deFord, Frank Belknap Long and Algernon Blackwood.

MINOR HAUNTINGS
Chilling Tales of Spectral Youth

ISBN 978 0 7123 5319 9 · 320 pages

From living dolls to spirits wandering in search of solace or vengeance, the ghostly youth is one of the most enduring phenomena of supernatural fiction, its roots stretching back into the realms of folklore and superstition.

Reviving obscure stories from Victorian periodicals alongside nail-biting episodes from master storytellers such as Elizabeth Gaskell, M. R. James and Margery Lawrence, this is a collection by turns enchanting, moving and thoroughly frightening.

QUEENS OF THE ABYSS
Lost Stories from the Women of the Weird

ISBN 978 0 7123 5391 5 · 352 pages

It is too often accepted that during the nineteenth and early twentieth centuries it was the male writers who developed and pushed the boundaries of the weird tale, with women writers following in their wake – but this is far from the truth.

This anthology presents the thrilling work of just a handful of writers crucial to the evolution of the genre, and revives lost authors of the early pulp magazines with material from the abyssal depths of the British Library vaults returning to the light for the first time since its original publication.

Delve in to see the darker side of *The Secret Garden* author Frances Hodgson Burnett and the sensitively-drawn nightmares of Marie Corelli and May Sinclair.

INTO THE LONDON FOG
Eerie Tales from the Weird City

ISBN 978 0 7123 5376 2 · 320 pages

As the smoky dark sweeps across the capital, strange stories emerge from the night. A séance reveals a ghastly secret in the murk of Regent's Canal. From south of the Thames come chilling reports of a spring-heeled spectre, and in Stoke Newington rumours abound of an opening to another world among the quiet alleys.

Waiting in the hazy streets are eerie tales from Charlotte Riddell, Lettice Galbraith and Violet Hunt, along with haunting pieces by Virginia Woolf, Arthur Machen, Sam Selvon and many more.

THE OUTCAST
and Other Tales by E. F. Benson

ISBN 978 0 7123 5386 1 · 288 pages

From deep in the British Library vaults emerges a new selection of E. F. Benson's most innovative, spine-tingling and satisfyingly dark 'spook stories'. Complete with an introduction exploring the fascinating story of Benson's life, and including the never-before-republished story 'Billy Comes Through', this volume hails the chilling return of an experimental master to whom writers of supernatural fiction have long been indebted.

ROARINGS FROM FURTHER OUT
Four Weird Novellas by Algernon Blackwood

ISBN 978 0 7123 5305 2 · 288 pages

Tightly wrought and deliciously suspenseful, Blackwood's novellas are quintessentially weird, pitching the reader into an uncanny space where the sublime forces of primordial Nature still dominate and in which the limits of the senses are uncertain. These are tales of powers beyond the frayed edges of human experience – tales which tug at the mind, and which prove as unsettling today as they first did over a century ago.

PROMETHEAN HORRORS
Classic Tales of Mad Science

ISBN 978 0 7123 5284 0 · 272 pages

Assembled here are ten thrilling tales of literature's most brilliant and misguided minds; minds that strive for the unnatural secrets of immortality, artificial life and the teleportation of matter; minds that must eventually grapple with the bitter cost of their obsessions.

From essential Gothic stories by Mary Shelley, E. T. A. Hoffmann and Edgar Allan Poe to later forays into the weird and psychedelic by E. Nesbit, H. P. Lovecraft and George Langelaan, the classic figure of the mad scientist is reanimated along with every untethered ambition and its calamitous consequences.

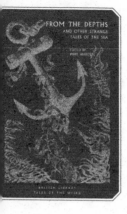

FROM THE DEPTHS
and Other Strange Tales of the Sea

ISBN 978 0 7123 5236 9 · 320 pages

In this anthology we see a thrilling spread of narratives; sailors are pitched against a nightmare from the depths, invisible to the naked eye; a German U-boat commander is tormented by an impossible transmission via Morse Code; a ship ensnares itself in the kelp of the Sargasso Sea and dooms a crew of mutineers, seemingly out of revenge for her lost captain...

THE PLATFORM EDGE
Uncanny Tales of the Railways

ISBN 978 0 7123 5203 1 · 304 pages

In this express service into the unknown, passengers join the jostling of the daily commute, a subway car disappears into another dimension without a trace, while a tragic derailment on a lonely hillside in the Alps torments the locals with its nightly repetition.

From the open railways of Europe and America to the pressing dark of the London Underground, *The Platform Edge* is the perfect travelling companion for unforgettable journeys into the supernatural.

SPIRITS OF THE SEASON
Christmas Hauntings

ISBN 978 0 7123 5252 9 · 320 pages

Festive cheer turns to maddening fear in this new collection of seasonal hauntings, which includes the best Christmas ghost stories from the 1860s to the 1940s.

The traditional trappings of the holiday are turned upside down as restless spirits disrupt the merry games of the living, Christmas trees teem with spiteful pagan presences and the Devil himself treads the boards at the village pantomime.

THE WEIRD TALES
of William Hope Hodgson

ISBN 978 0 7123 5233 8 · 240 pages

Abandon the safety of the familiar with ten nerve-wracking episodes of horror penned by master of atmosphere and suspense, William Hope Hodgson.

From encounters with abominations at sea to fireside tales of otherworldly forces recounted by occult detective Carnacki, this new selection offers the most unsettling of Hodgson's weird stories, guaranteed to terrorise the steeliest of constitutions.

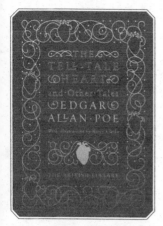

The Tell-Tale Heart
and Other Tales by Edgar Allan Poe
ISBN 978 0 7123 5754 8 · 208 pages

Fearsome Fairies
Haunting Tales of the Fae
ISBN 978 0 7123 5430 1 · 336 pages

The Little Blue Flames
and Other Uncanny Tales
by A. M. Burrage
ISBN 978 0 7123 5412 7 · 256 pages

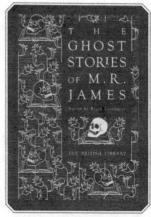

The Ghost Stories of M. R. James
ISBN 978 0 7123 5250 5 · 208 pages

BRITISH LIBRARY TALES OF THE WEIRD

We welcome any suggestions, corrections or feedback you may have, and will aim to respond to all items addressed to the following:

The Editor (Tales of the Weird), British Library Publishing,
The British Library, 96 Euston Road, London NW1 2DB

We also welcome enquiries through our Twitter account, @BL_Publishing.